# THE BOOK OF TBILISI

Edited by Gvantsa Jobava
& Becca Parkinson

First published in Great Britain in 2017 by Comma Press
commapress.co.uk

Copyright © remains with the authors, translators
This collection copyright © Comma Press, 2017.

All rights reserved.

'Patagonia' was first published in Georgian in *Tasmanian Tiger* (2013). 'Uncle Evgeni's Game' was first published in *Arili* (2014). 'Precision' was first published in *Open the Door* (2013). 'On Facebook' was first published in *On Facebook* (2014). 'Balba-Tso' was first published in *Literaturili Gazeti* (2012). 'Tsa' was first published in *Arili* (2014). 'A Bronx Tale a la Gold Quarter' was first published in *Literaturili Palitra* (2014). 'Dad After Mum' was first published in *Literaturuli Gazeti* (2014). 'Peridé' was first published in *Literaturili Gazeti* (2017).

The moral rights of the contributors to be identified as the authors of this Work have been asserted in accordance with the Copyright Designs and Patents Act 1988.

The stories in this anthology are entirely works of fiction. The names, characters and incidents portrayed in them are entirely the work of the authors' imagination. Any resemblance to actual persons, living or dead, events, organisations or localities, is entirely coincidental. Any characters that appear, or claim to be based on real ones are intended to be entirely fictional. The opinions of the authors and the editors are not those of the publisher.

A CIP catalogue record of this book is available from the British Library.
ISBN: 1910974315
ISBN-13: 9781910974315

This book is published with the support of the Georgian National Book Center and the Ministry of Culture and Monument Protection of Georgia.

The publisher gratefully acknowledges assistance from Arts Council England.

Printed and bound in England by CPI Group (UK) Ltd, Croydon CR0 4YY

## *Praise for The Book of Tbilisi*

'If you're fortunate enough to visit Georgia, you'll be struck by its beauty and raw grandeur, the churches and wine cellars and icon stores, the open generosity of those you encounter, the language and the unique shapes of its alphabet. If you're paying attention, you'll be aware of what Tbilisi has endured, and of its rich literary tradition in poetry and fiction which is now being embraced by a new generation. This anthology acts as an introduction to a literature quite neglected by the Anglophone world. In these works we find the self-effacing wit of the survivor, hard-bitten but never cynical. Or, if jaded (and with good reason) underpinned by a deep and humbling spirituality. There is a range of voice and style here, but the language consistently has the direct, clean and unadorned quality of great fiction, which suits the subtlety and complexity of the lives examined, the nuance and the subtext of the past's pervasive presence. We feel the hopes and the fears of the narrators and protagonists, the State's broken contracts and prevarications. Ultimately these are stories of the resilience of the human soul.'
– Luke Kennard, author of *The Transition*

'Far from the glamorous buzz of touristic Tbilisi, these heartbreakingly realistic stories tell of ordinary lives turned upside down. From social neglect to social media absurdity, we meet the victims and the survivors – but where all seems lost, small acts of human kindness offer hope. Like a decent Georgian table wine these stories linger in the mind, earthy and rather raw and intensely felt.'
– Anthea Nicholson, author of *The Banner of Passing Clouds*

'A soaring, searing collection – important new stories that are sure to live long in the memory.'
– Eley Williams, author of *Attrib*

# Contents

| | |
|---|---|
| INTRODUCTION<br>Gvantsa Jobava | vii |
| UNCLE EVGENI'S GAME<br>Dato Kardava<br>Translated by Nino Kiguradze | 1 |
| ON FACEBOOK<br>Gela Chkvanava<br>Translated by Tamar Japaridze | 19 |
| PRECISION<br>Erekle Deisadze<br>Translated by Philip Price | 39 |
| PERIDÉ<br>Zviad Kvaratskhelia<br>Translated by Mary Childs | 49 |
| TSA<br>Iva Pezuashvili<br>Translated by Mary Childs | 57 |
| FLOOD<br>Shota Iatashvili<br>Translated by George Siharulidze | 85 |

| | |
|---|---:|
| DAD AFTER MUM<br>Rusudan Rukhadze<br>Translated by Tamar Japaridze | 93 |
| A BRONX TALE A LA GOLD QUARTER<br>Lado Kilasonia<br>Translated by Maya Kiasashvili | 107 |
| BALBA-TSO<br>Ina Archuashvili<br>Translated by Philip Price | 117 |
| PATAGONIA<br>Bacho Kvirtia<br>Translated by Nino Kiguradze | 125 |
| About the Authors | 137 |
| About the Translators | 143 |

# Introduction

WHAT CAN THE 31-YEAR-OLD co-editor of this book, born during the last decade of the Soviet rule, in a republic struggling towards freedom, tell you about the wider history of her native, capital city? Quite a lot, as it happens! For the identity of Tbilisi is a heady mix of myth, historical conflict, and geological fortuity that even its younger citizens can appreciate. To begin with, Tbilisi's worst-kept secret is its ability to forever rise from the ashes, to recover and reconstruct itself, to recapture its former glories, even when, through conquest and external rule, all seems lost. It's one of the reasons residents readily believe any number of myths and legends about the place. One of these miraculous stories tells how the city was originally founded:

Back at the start of the Middle Ages, the territory we now call Tbilisi was covered with dense woodland. According to the legend, King Vakhtang I Gorgasali of Georgia, ruling in the second half of the 5$^{th}$ century, went hunting with his men in the forests here. During the hunt the king wounded a roe deer with an arrow. The animal limped away into the dense thicket, and the king's men ran after it, following the drops of blood it left behind. This trail led the men to a boiling hot spring. There, they witnessed how the water bubbling out of the ground healed the wounded doe, as if it contained some magical properties, and the doe, now recovered, disappeared into the forest again. The men related this miracle to their king and showed him the spot where it had happened. So impressed was he with this tale, and with the hot sulphuric springs, that

# INTRODUCTION

the king ordered his new capital city to be built in that very spot.

Georgia, the country that Tbilisi now stands as the capital of, sits in the heart of the Caucasus mountain range, right on the border of the Orient and the Occident, at the crossroads of Europe and Asia. The country's favourable geopolitical location was the main reason for our ancestors' obstreperous and worrisome existence; the long, dramatic history of Tbilisi, its many conquests and resurrections, was largely a consequence of the country's strategic, geographic importance. For many centuries the city has been the object of rivalry between various invaders, from the Persians to the Byzantines, from the Khazars to the Arabs, from the Seljuk Turks to the Mongols and the Ottomans. On top of all this, Tbilisi managed to survive 70 years of Soviet rule, and only saw its independence regained 26 years ago. So don't be surprised, when visiting the city, to meet a younger generation that is defined by its sense of spiritual freedom, its democratic frame of mind, its sensitivity to issues such as gender equality, or religious tolerance; don't be surprised to find a generation actively engaged in the struggles against homophobia and xenophobia; because this is a generation born out of new-found freedoms – freedoms we don't take for granted. But this spirit of tolerance is perhaps a longer standing Tbilisi tradition, not unique to the current younger generation. Historically Tbilisi has always been a diverse, multicultural city; visitors should not be surprised to come across a Mosque, a Synagogue, an Armenian Gregorian Church or a Catholic Church while strolling through the old parts of city, even though Tbilisi is the capital of an Orthodox Christian country. One of the most famous medieval kings of Georgia, David the Builder, ruling in the $12^{th}$ century, tried to rebuild Tbilisi (having been recently destroyed by Turks) as the capital city of the whole of 'Transcaucasia', a capital for all the ethnicities living in the region.

## INTRODUCTION

Evidence of this multicultural past can be seen in Tbilisi's highly eclectic architecture, although perhaps the most popular aspects of the Old Town, for many tourists, is the charming, closely-packed two- or three-storey residential houses built in the 19th century. Here, elements of classical and local architecture are interwoven seamlessly, in the houses' façades, adorned as they are with elaborate, wooden balconies. Walking through the entrance halls of these buildings, and into courtyards that from the street you would never have imagined, is a revelation. This is what one of the outstanding modern Georgian writers, Aka Morchiladze, writes about it:

> Tbilisi is a city of streets full of wonders and puzzles: you can go through a dark, cool arch and find yourself in an incredible yard. The arch itself might have the look of a Stalinist era monument, but beyond it you might find yourself in a courtyard dappled with acacia trees, built by some Swiss architect in a pseudo-classical style a century and a half before. And beyond that might lie the ruins of a medieval brick church bell-tower, overlooked by a wooden balcony typical of Tbilisi's old townhouses, or a pavilion with corbels made out of plaster Atlases, with an outdoor barbeque beside it. And what can you discover going through the creaking iron gates from that yard to the neighbouring one? Some new mystery and wonder!

Thus, it is often difficult for visitors in Tbilisi to work out where they are, stylistically – in Asia or Europe. The city, built on the hilly banks of the M't'kvari (the River Kura), is overlooked by the ancient Narikala fortress, which has a mix of Persian, Umayyad, Mongolian and early renaissance heritage. Below lies a similar cocktail of contrasting ingredients: the symmetric, oriental domes of the bathhouses; the ancient

# INTRODUCTION

Legvtakhevi waterfall sunk into the middle of a bustling, modern city centre; bridges, both old and modern, crisscrossing the river. Restaurants entertain their guests with folk songs and traditional Georgian dance, in between European-style bars, cafés and nightclubs; Orthodox Christian temples, packed to the rafters with church-goers at weekends, stand either side of districts that have effectively become one enormous "hotel" for the city's myriads of tourists; cracked and neglected old houses, inclining this way and that, jostle beside examples of daring modern architecture that continually cause debate among the city's residents. Indeed, no-one is surprised to see protestors occasionally taking to the streets with placards demanding that we *'Keep the City's Traditional Looks'* or *'Preserve our Greenery and Oxygen!'*

Tbilisians are a fiery-tempered people, by reputation; we keep our calm for a while, but then erupt like volcanoes. We are keenly engaged in current politics and closely follow the games played by politicians. This temperament might also be the result of our rather dramatic recent history: living under 70 years of Communist oppression, struggling for the freedom we now cherish, and latterly maintaining that freedom. The most famous flashpoints in this recent history were the huge demonstrations of anti-Soviet sentiment in 1956, 1978, and 1989, which were quickly and brutally suppressed, in the first and latter cases taking the lives of many courageous young Georgians.

Nor was peace restored quickly in the aftermath of the break-up of the Soviet Union in 1991/92. This was a time of significant instability for the country, followed by a coup d'état overthrowing Georgia's first democratically elected president – a coup during which half of the downtown area of Tbilisi was left in ruins. 1992-1993 witnessed a new war – between Russia and Georgia – for one of the oldest regions of the country, Abkhazia. After this, Tbilisi became a battlefield for

## INTRODUCTION

confrontations between various Mafiosi clans and illegal business entrepreneurs. Crime and corruption became rampant at most levels of society. Escalating unemployment dragged large swathes of the population into extreme poverty. I often hear from my parents' generation that this latter crisis came with a positive side, however: it brought the people together; those who could afford to opened up their doors to the needy, helping them through the hard times by sharing what they had. Nevertheless, many of Tbilisi's most impoverished citizens were embittered, and in many cases morally corrupted, by the whole experience.

Ultimately, the disillusionment of this era forced people onto the streets with a popular movement that culminated in the *Rose Revolution* in November 2003, overthrowing the government of the time. Since then, Tbilisi has enjoyed more stability and an improved economy, although in 2008 war with Russia broke out again – this time over South Ossetia and Abkhazia – resulting in an influx of refugees for the city. To this day, both Abkhazia and South Ossetia – undeniable regions of Georgia – are still occupied by Russians. In fact, in 2008, rumours spread that Russia was going to target Tbilisi itself, as their troops were getting nearer. Some citizens even fled. But Tbilisi is a city of miracles, and many believe that it was indeed a miracle the Russians didn't attack the city that year. Who knows? Maybe they're right.

Currently Tbilisi is one of the most stable, peaceful, and prosperous places in the region, with miraculously increasing numbers of tourists from all over the world, each year.

How did we manage to survive? Maybe it was thanks to our creative nature. Even at the height of those anti-Soviet demonstrations, cordoned off by Russian tanks on all sides, the young Georgians would sing, dance and recite poems, staring into the eyes of their oppressors. Georgia is often called 'the land of poets'. You'd be hard pressed to find a Georgian who

# INTRODUCTION

hasn't, at one stage in his or her life, written a poem. Our writers and our literature have always had a great influence on shaping our social awareness and cultural outlook. The mother tongue has always been held in the highest regard. So, during the Soviet era, the whole nation fought unanimously to maintain the status of Georgian as the official, national language.

The original Georgian script is a legacy of Egyptian, Phoenician and Sumerian origins (and in 2016 was named in UNESCO's 'Representative List of the Intangible Cultural Heritage of Humanity'). It can be traced back to the 4th century. The oldest surviving manuscript, *The Martyrdom of the Holy Queen Shushanik*, written by a priest Jacob Tsurtaveli, is considered to be the first hagiographic novel written in Georgian. This book became the principal basis of the cultural, and political identity of the country. It encouraged the studies of the surviving manuscripts of various kinds. At present there are 11,000 examples of these early Georgian manuscripts housed in Georgia and libraries all over the world.

In the 12th century, Shota Rustaveli, the great Georgian poet and thinker, created his famous poem 'The Knight in the Panther's Skin', considered a masterpiece of medieval literature by many experts. The poem has been translated into many languages, and remains a powerful source of inspiration for contemporary poets, having the status of a kind of 'second Bible' for the Georgian people.

In 1709, King Vakhtang VI, himself a scholar, philosopher, translator and poet, established the first printing house in Tbilisi, which was also Georgia's first publishing house. This event marked the beginning of a new literary era for the country, starting with the publication of the Georgian chronicles, edited and overseen by the king himself, which told the country's history from the Dark Ages to the Early Modern Era.

# INTRODUCTION

For the first part of the 19th century, Tbilisi was home to Georgian romanticists Alexander Chavchavadze, Grigol Orbeliani and Nikoloz Baratashvili. In the 1840s, writers such as Giorgi Eristavi, Lavrenti Ardaziani, Daniel Chonkadze and others, laid the foundations for Georgian critical realism; while in the 1860s, the literary arena was dominated by the so-called 'Tergdaleulebi' (St Petersburg-educated 'men of letters'), under the leadership of the great Georgian writer and prominent public figure Ilia Chavchavadze (often given the title of the 'Father of Nation'). Chavchavadze is credited with taking both Georgia's literature and its critical thinking to a new level. Having spearheaded the revival of the Georgian nationalist movement, championed the use of the Georgian language, campaigned for the autonomy of the Georgian national church, and ultimately been canonised by the Georgian Orthodox and Apostolic Church (as 'Saint Ilia the Righteous'), it is no surprise that, almost a century later, he became an iconic source of inspiration for the 1989 anti-Soviet protests.

The 1880s, saw the emergence of great poets such as Vazha-Pshavela (whose depictions of the natural landscape have no equal in Georgian literature) and Galaktion Tabidze (whose verse climbed to the summit of what poetry can do in terms of harmony, rhythm, colour, and tone). The beginning of the 20th century saw a new wave of great short story writers and novelists: Alexandre Kazbegi, Davit Kldiashvili, Vasil Barnov, Mikheil Javakhishvili, Konstantine Gamsakhurdia and Otar Chiladze. In 1917, a group of Georgian symbolists known as the 'Tsisperkantselebi' (including Titsian Tabidze, Paolo Iashvili, Valerian Gaprindashvili and others) famously moved from Kutaisi, the artistic centre of the country at the time, to Tbilisi, bringing an entire poetry scene to the city. To this day, fantastic poets like Besik Kharanauli, Vakhtang Javakhadze and Tariel Chanturia continue to live and create in Tbilisi, discovering new poetic forms in the Georgian language

# INTRODUCTION

and influencing the way the language is used by other poets, and writers more generally.

During the Soviet period, an important school of translators developed as well that saw an enormous number of world classics and modern masterpieces translated into Georgian. Between 1921 and 1990, a total of 93,659 books were published in Georgian, a high proportion of them in translation. After the break-up of the Soviet Union, independent, private publishing houses started to sprout up in Tbilisi replacing centralised, state ones. And although the industrial scale of the Soviet era publishing has not been maintained, the city's new breed of indie publishing houses are making a remarkable contribution to the literary health of the nation.

The Georgian language belongs to a distinct group of the Kartvelian languages spoken only by Georgians. This linguistic independence is perhaps one of the reasons why many of the great treasures of Georgian literature have yet to be discovered by the rest of the world. However the current, groundbreaking generation of Georgian writers is beginning to cross borders. *The Book of Tbilisi* offers us a glimpse of this generation, with stories by ten of the city's most exciting young writers: Bacho Kvirtia, Dato Kardava, Erekle Deisadze, Gela Chkvanava, Ina Archuashvili, Shota Iatashvili, Iva Pezuashvili, Lado Kilasonia, Rusudan Rukhadze and Zviad Kvaratskhelia. Each story is in some way a continuation of previous Georgian literary traditions. Each one offers a snapshot of life in present-day Tbilisi, the city's customs and traditions, and the many complex dynamics at play between its citizens – from the corrupting influence of poverty, to the possibilities of love and friendship, from the manipulations of the media, to the impact of petty bureaucracy on real people's lives. We also see how much of Georgian society is still deeply rooted in the traditions of family life, which have both positive and negative outcomes for the stories' characters. Parents and older generations are highly revered by Georgian people, who take great care of them ('Dad after Mum'), and many Georgians still live in extended family environments, where several generations co-exist peacefully or otherwise ('Tsa'). At times the problems of gender inequality are still manifest, and we still witness examples of physical and mental abuse in the home ('Patagonia'). In the 1990s, during one of the hardest periods in Georgian history, family life came under enormous pressure. In a society struggling for survival, the experience of seeing your own children go hungry was unbearable; the domestic environment became a battleground. Often these tensions expressed themselves through psychological disorders ('Flood'). It was during this time that Georgian women found their greatest voice: the majority of Georgia's women made it their mission to defend and support their families themselves: they went out into the streets and became vendors, or went abroad seeking better paid jobs to support their families back home. As for the men, many came back from the two wars psychologically broken, often falling prey to alcoholism, depression, and lethargy, and constituting an aggressive, violent new side to society ('Patagonia'). These days more and more Georgian women enjoy complete independence; they are successful in their careers and can support themselves and their children easily; also, luckily, more and more of our men are adopting progressive attitudes and subscribe to the principle of fair democracy within the household. However, the wars of the last few decades and the hardships they've caused, as well as the economic emigration, have had a huge impact on Georgian families, destroying households; many children were orphaned or made homeless. Some went out into the streets to beg, and can still be seen there ('Precision').

In this anthology, you will hear ten voices from a generation that grew up during these decades of hardship; a

## INTRODUCTION

generation that experienced the unmasked cruelty of the world around them, and managed to adapt to an almost endless series of changes; a generation that contributed to the collapse of the old system, coped with the consequences of that collapse, and invested all its energies into the building of a new one. Furthermore, these authors in particular struggled and survived as representatives of a new, open society, in order to hold a mirror up to the city and the country they live in.

The ten stories selected for this book offer a kind of literary guidebook to an outside world that used to be very remote. They tell you about the human challenges of living in a small country struggling, daily, to maintain its place on the map; a country where people are happy to welcome visitors from the rest of Europe visa-free, and equally happy to see its students go abroad and study at the best universities in Europe; a country that's proud of its work ethic and the high standards of its services, and happy to maintain its unique blend of both European and non-European traditions. As Georgians, we are delighted with every new, progressive step the country takes, but will never forget that our northern neighbour is irritated by our progress, and seems intent to start reuniting post-Soviet countries under its rule again. Such is the destiny of the small country struggling for its independence, on the doorstep of a once-dominant empire. The citizens of this country are ordinary people, and some of them you'll get to know (and perhaps even sympathise with) in the stories that follow, for they are like-minded souls, living not far from you, and who, like you, believe in miracles sometimes.

Gvantsa Jobava
Tbilisi, November 2017

*Translated by Tamar Japaridze*

# Uncle Evgeni's Game

## Dato Kardava

### Translated by Nino Kiguradze

JOURNALISTS WERE LIKE CIGARETTE ash and the news desk was like a dirty ashtray that no one bothered to empty till it was full. The office floor was also covered with cigarette ash, *literally*. The walls, which were painted half in blue, half in white, were darkened with cigarette stains like poorly healed ulcers on a patient's body.

When Redhead appeared, the ashtray had been newly emptied out. The newspaper needed new employees: green, inexperienced trainees with modest ambitions, willing to work hard, and only complain timidly if their meagre salaries were paid late, or not at all. The sort of employees who wouldn't pluck anyone's eyes, but would endure all this at least until the office became full again with burnt out and easily disposable journalists, who'd then be told: 'If being here doesn't work for you, find somewhere else.'

'It's just another ordinary Tbilisi newspaper,' the news editor said, scratching his hairy neck, as he showed Redhead around. 'At times it's grey and other times full of colour,' he explained. 'Horoscopes, humorous cartoons, psychological quizzes, recipes for the fasting period, advice from lawyers... we cover *all sorts*. 'What advice would you give us, Father? Why Brother? Or what we should know about our legal rights.' And so on. In other words, it's just another newspaper where you can publish almost anything. What's important is it has to be said with *passion*!'

'With passion?' Redhead asked, warily.

'Of course!' the news editor raised his voice. 'You know… with an interesting twist!'

Outside it was snowing. Redhead was surprised to be seeing snow in Tbilisi in October. Other residents seemed confused by it too. Only reckless children could be seen running around in it joyfully trying to catch snowflakes with their mouths.

\*

Like most men, Baldy looked old for his age. He lit up his cigarette and asked Redhead what it was that couldn't wait until the morning. In reply, Redhead said he wanted a story, a real one with blood, corpses – in other words, something scandalous.

Baldy took him to his neighbour, a former investigator who had seen a lot in his time, having worked for both the Soviet and Georgian police forces.

The man's name was written on the door: *Evgeni Samosia*. Or was it *Jarmusia*? It was dark in the hallway and Redhead couldn't quite make out what it said.

'Beer?' asked Uncle Evgeni. 'Everything is better with a beer!' he added, burping. Redhead gazed past him at the television where anime characters were chasing each other in circles and yelling.

The former police officer wore a wig. He was as pale as a corpse, and his eyes were the same shade of light blue as the faded tattoos that adorned his arms, shoulders, chest and neck; they were so light, it was impossible to make out what they were supposed to be tattoos of. On his bare feet he wore pointy moccasins, which wobbled back and forth as he walked. He headed to the kitchen to get glasses and turned the TV volume down on his way. 'Uncle Evgeni was a great man,' Baldy whispered.

'I will tell the story as it was, and you can put it in order later,' Uncle Evgeni began as he re-lit his almost finished cigarette. Redhead pressed record on his Dictaphone.

## Track 01: Uncle Evgeni

'We were in my office one night, my two co-workers and me, when the guard poked his head round the door. "Just got a call from the hospital," he said. "They had to operate on some guy during the night – not a serious operation – but they couldn't calm him down afterwards. He was hysterical about seeing his wife. *"Where is she?"* he was shouting. "Why hasn't she come to see me? What if something has happened to her?" He wouldn't calm down, so they called it in. A man who's just had surgery deserves a visit from his wife!

'"Go and find out what happened," I said to my co-worker. "Ask the guy where we should start looking for his wife." Shortly after I went to the hospital too. The doctor told me part of his intestines had come out – about ten feet of them.'

'Intestines? You mean appendix, surely!' Baldy interrupted.
'Intestines!'
'Are you sure you're using the right word?'
'The right word is... asshole!' Redhead got involved.
'His asshole had come out! How?' Baldy patted his behind.
'That's what I asked too!' said Uncle Evgeni. 'How could it have come out? It's not like a wallet. What does it mean? The doctor said he must have lifted something heavy.'

I sent two men to his house, they talked to his neighbours, but nobody knew anything.'

## Track 02: Male Neighbour

'How did you hear about that one, guys? Ha! You're journalists I guess? And why do you want to know? It was so long ago…

I can't even remember. I couldn't tell you the exact year, but I'll never forget the story. His name was Yuri. He was a young man, around 28, maybe 30. A couple of years older than me. He hadn't long graduated from university, where he'd studied chemistry and was now working as an engineer in an amber-producing factory. When he moved here, he had a wife and two kids – such unfortunate kids. By the way, I don't believe what they said about it in the papers. Something must have happened; otherwise how could a man do something so crazy? I saw him the morning it happened; there was nothing unusual about him, he seemed in a good mood. I was having a quick drink with my friend Jora Kalicev at his shoe repair shop – Jora was a good man. Yuri came in, said hello, said no to a beer and handed Jora his wife's shoes. Women still wear those kind of shoes – I can't remember what they're called these days – back then they were called "Frankfurts". Anyway, I can't remember whether the heel was broken or bent. Jora didn't take money from Yuri, instead that unfortunate guy – whom I pitied a great deal – gave Jora a bottle of Stolichnaya vodka. He left without drinking any himself. I haven't seen him since then, he was arrested shortly after. I can't remember anything bad about him. Once or twice, we even played dominos together in the yard. I knew his wife too. Well, I wouldn't say I *knew* her exactly, she was neighbourly with my mum. She would ask to borrow some oil, or money, those types of things. She was a beautiful girl. Not just beautiful, she was different. I don't know how to say this but… she was majestic? They weren't suited to each other. I remember even Jora, who has passed away since, said this girl must be strange otherwise why on earth would she want to marry him?'

## Track 01: Uncle Evgeni

'I knew Yuri from Sori. Not just him, I knew everybody there. I knew some from the streets, others from the factory. Yuri had graduated from Tbilisi Technical University. People spoke well of him at the factory. When I got to the hospital, he was lying on his stomach, unable to turn.

'"Greetings friend," I said. I think he recognised me. He told me he didn't know where his wife was, and that she wasn't here to see him, even in his condition. "Where could she be?" I asked, looking at him. I sat down beside him on his bed.

"Perhaps she went to see her relatives," he said and named some village. "I sent someone over there already, all in vain."'

## Track 03: Aunt, Village Mukhati

'Everyone looked out for that unfortunate girl – including my poor sister and my brother-in-law. She didn't listen to anyone or consider their advice. She just took off with him. My heart breaks for her! She was an only child, pampered. I wish she hadn't taken off from our house. My sister tried to distance them. She thought: if they didn't see each other her feelings would go away. But they didn't go away. Do those kinds of feelings ever go away? The neighbours saw them taking off at dawn. Eka was sprinting and jumping over whatever was in her way, they were laughing about it, the neighbour told me. She left behind a couple of diaries. She wrote some things in them – poetry, I guess, written by a silly, stupid girl. She used to write about the moon, love, flowers. That boy drove her crazy. My cousin tried to find out about that unmentionable horror. Apparently, he had been expelled from the army, declared insane, and spent time in an institution. There were rumours about him playing cards and hanging out at a graveyard, but our silly girl insisted that it was all just rumours and lies. Lies. Even the rumour about him being insane was a lie. She said he had pretended to be insane so he wouldn't have to be a soldier. If it wasn't just a lie, there, she got served.'

## Track 01: Uncle Evgeni

'When I came out in the hallway, the nurse told me that Kainidze had been asking for his passport and money. She'd accidently overheard him asking the assistant nurse. The assistant nurse told me he was devising some wretched plan. He hadn't slept all night and he wouldn't stop talking about his money and his passport. Then my co-workers brought a picture of the missing woman. She was really beautiful.'

'Was she really that beautiful?' Redhead interrupted again. 'Like Angelina Jolie or something?'

'More so!'

'How?'

'Well, an Angelina Jolie with a larger chest!'

'Wait, are big boobs a good thing?'

Uncle Evgeni put his hands inside his robe.

'A woman without boobs is like a bed without a pillow!'

'But what about ass?'

'There was nothing missing. She had everything! She was a woman of many possessions, but her house was empty. The neighbours said they weren't just poor, they were really struggling. Their house had little more than a couple of chairs, a table, a metal bed frame and a black and white TV.'

## Track 04: Female Neighbour

They used to fight every evening, but I don't believe it ever reached a level of physical violence. At least, I didn't notice anything on her face, hands or body. They would smash the dishes. She was a strong girl, she could hold her own. I'm not sure what they were fighting about. She even quit working. She had a good job; she worked at a dairy or a meat deli. I can't remember exactly, but he made her quit. At the end she was working at a daycare, but he didn't even want that, even though they were really struggling financially. When they moved here, they didn't even own a bed. I gave them a metal bed frame and they used to sleep on that, without a mattress. They didn't even have a table. Then they slowly started to buy things. But they were never comfortable. They had no one who could help, and nobody came to visit them. I used to think what kind of mother she must have had. That boy didn't have any family either. He grew up without a father and his mother was in a nursing home in the suburbs of Tbilisi. The girl, as I said before, was abandoned by her relatives. That's how it usually happens in the village. "Why didn't you listen to us, why did you bring shame to our family?" There you go, they have all suffered for it. What more could I? I am trying to forget this story, I thought I *had* forgotten about it. I wish you hadn't reminded me.'

## Track 01: Uncle Evgeni

'I sent out a search party into the forests surrounding Tbilisi. We even tracked along the Mtkvari River almost the whole way to the Azerbaijani border. We looked at the railroads. But nothing.

'"He probably murdered her," one of the neighbours told me. "He was always shouting at her; he probably beat her and sometimes wouldn't let her leave the house." Meanwhile the woman's relatives started to gather. I feared they would stone him to death. I told my men to smuggle him out of the hospital and hide him in a safe house.

'Before sunrise, I scoped out the flat again. Everything in it looked like it did in any other family home. Clothes were in the closet; shoes were placed on a shoe rack. In short, the flat was orderly. I left nothing unchecked even under the floorboards. Suddenly I realised something: why was the house *so* clean and tidy? If the woman had plans to run away, why had she spent time scrubbing the floors? It looked as if someone had cleaned the place very meticulously. I pressured him for five days to confess: "You ass! How could you murder your wife!" At first he acted oblivious, then he seemed to be outraged. "How dare you accuse me of such a thing?" Then he laughed and cried, pretending to lose his mind. After the second or third day the test results came back from forensics. In the water they had taken, they found blood. Just by looking at it you couldn't tell whose; all the same, we had a good forensic scientist. When I saw the results, I wouldn't leave him alone. On the fifth day he broke down.'

## Track 05: Former Prosecutor

'How could I forget my first job assignment, especially a job so horrific? During the court hearing, people were passing out in the conference room, others in the office. I remember we had to replace the court reporter. It was very hard for me to hear it too. I was only 22 or 23 at the time. I had just graduated from university and, having an honours degree, they put me forward for the prosecution team. Fortune is a funny thing. Why did it have to be me? It was a very dark case, especially being my first one. At first I regretted getting into this profession, but after a while I became used to it. No, from a prosecutor's perspective, it wasn't a tough case to crack. Once it was in my hands, there was nothing to investigate; he had already confessed his crime. It's just that the case itself was horrific. For a while I considered trying him under the 111E code (premeditated murder due to unexpected uneasy mental circumstances) but I quickly changed my mind. The story of the kids was the breaking point. I was severely disturbed by this aspect of it. Under no circumstances could there be any talk of a less severe sentence. I asked for the highest form of punishment. Execution. And even though the newspapers carried the story – that the sentence had been carried out in full – some people were still saying that he hadn't been executed; that he'd got off on a 'Jaba Amnesty';[1] or that he'd been seen alive and well in Russia, and so on. It was all nonsense! I know for sure he that he was executed. I had kept some of the material from the trial. Of course, I also have a copy of his account. I can't give it to you, but I can let you see it. You can copy it, or I could read it to you and you could write it down. Are you already writing it down? That's fine:

'I was watching television when she walked by me, I wrapped my arm around her and pulled her towards my lap. They were showing the movie *Taming of the Shrew*, not the one with Celentano, the one filmed earlier with Elizabeth Taylor. She pushed me away and started arguing with me. I was in a good mood and wouldn't leave her alone. I wanted to make up. I told her, "Look, love can make you do anything," but she pushed me again and started cursing. Eventually she said, "Don't start up about how you love me!" "Do you have any doubts?' I asked and smiled. She said she hated me. I couldn't think of anything to say. Then I saw the children and asked her, aren't they the fruit of our love? Perhaps I said something else, I can't remember exactly but this was the basic gist. The kids were there too, they were either playing or studying I can't recall. "The kids you are looking at aren't even yours," she said suddenly. "Then whose kids are they?" I asked with a smile. "Which one? The older one or the younger one?" She said this far too quickly, too instinctively and naively that I thought she couldn't have made it up that fast. I don't know what came over me. I remember grabbing her and smashing her against the toilet, breaking her spine. I dismembered her right there in the bathtub and when it was dark I buried her underneath a nearby building, which was still under construction. When I came back I scrubbed the floors, changed my clothes and when I had finished everything I started to feel sick. I thought the sick feeling would go away but nothing changed. I started to feel so sick that I called the ambulance, telling them my intestines had come out.'

Track 01: Uncle Evgeni

'Chikatilo!' Baldy put his hands on his head. Uncle Evgeni lit a cigarette and took a sip from his beer.

'If I had told the whole story they would have stoned him. The crowd was gathering around the Unit. They knew something terrible had happened. And I knew for sure that if I told them what had happened, they would snatch him and stone him to death. The man who had come in from the Ministry was pressuring me into admitting the murderer had run away and that I was concealing it.

'I discovered the body at 2am at night. Not a body but bodies. He had killed his children too, but he hadn't confessed it during the investigation or after the trial. He insisted that he hadn't touched the children. What did it matter that they weren't his children. "The children didn't do anything to me? Why would I murder them?" he asked. He had buried the woman and the children together. I took pictures and made a portfolio.

'I took out every part of the body from the ground, I swear on my father's soul. When they put all the body parts together, they were surprised that I had been able to find every part.'

'What do you mean put together? It's not like it's Lego pieces,' Baldy asked, as he got up to go to the bathroom. Uncle Evgeni told him not to sit on the toilet, because it was cracked. Then he turned to Redhead and asked him, 'Where did I stop?'

'When they were surprised at the morgue!'

'Not only at the morgue. I placed Kainidze in a solitary cell, in one of our safehouses. I thought that was it, that the main job was done, but little did I know the worst was still to come. The man who had been sent from the Ministry was insisting that I had known the murdered woman. That I had won her in a game of cards against Kainidze. There were stories about such things going round the city at the time.'

'Won a woman in a game of cards?' Redhead interrupted. 'How can you win a woman, is she a chip?'

At this point, Baldy returned.

'When a person loses everything, and he doesn't have anything else left to bet...' started Baldy, 'then he bets his wife. If he loses he has to let his wife get screwed!'

'What do you mean screw?'

'No way! No chance!'

'Well if he doesn't want to let his wife get screwed, he has to murder her instead.'

'Murder?'

'Should I continue?' asked Uncle Evgeni.

They both said yes.

'"I don't know either the man nor the woman," I yelled at the guys from the Ministry. "I don't even know how to play cards! Have you lost your minds?" Nobody believed me. They told me to come see them in the evening. There, I told them everything, how it had all happened. I didn't hide anything. I don't know if they believed me or not but, they let me go.'

## Track 06: Neighbourhood Boy

'Varketili was a new neighbourhood. It was under construction with many houses still not finished. They were building many apartments at the same time. Some apartments were completed but empty, others had residents already living in them, some still had cranes around them, and so on. You couldn't find a blade of grass or a single tree. I could only recall three colours from the days of my childhood: brown, from stone-like dirt; black from the newly laid asphalt where our feet used to get stuck; and blue from the sky. Back then, a child's main form of entertainment consisted of running round construction sites and playing: tag, hide and seek... Our toys were complementary to the situation too: empty metal boxes, wires, pieces of iron, used nails, bobbins from unknown sources, electrodes, broken tars, which at times we used to chew or melt to make sticks.

'We saw our first dead person there, at the building site. A construction worker had fallen from the 6$^{th}$ floor. Everyone ran towards him, but as for us, we were there already – we always played on the site. They wouldn't let us at him though, they were trying to get rid of us. I managed to squeeze past some of them, but I couldn't make much out. It turned out to be our schoolmate's father. On the day of the burial, the teacher took us to the funeral. That was the first time I saw a dead person. My mother had warned me to put my head down and not to look at the dead or I would have a nightmare. I was planning not to, but at the last minute before leaving, I looked at him. I remember the dead person had his head wrapped in white cloths or bandages and only his gray face was showing. Then I really saw my classmate's dead father in a dream with blood oozing from his white cloth. When I told the story later to neighbourhood kids, one of the girls told me someone else would also die now. I remember being very frightened. At night, when I lay in bed I couldn't sleep: it's all I could think about. Then it happened, in our neighbourhood, a man murdered his wife and kids… a boy and a girl, siblings. The girl was little, but the brother was around our age. Once or twice we had played football together. Our parents hid it from us, they wouldn't tell us what had happened, but somehow we found out. I remember not exactly pitying them but being frightened. It wasn't just me, we were all afraid to even go near that building. One time my older brother insisted he recognised the window of their basement home and he told us to look inside if we dared. Two or three of us dared to go. It was a small window with a sun-shaped grill, with iron rays spreading out from the centre. I was so frightened I couldn't see anything: just infinite darkness. My heart was racing. It was so hot that the asphalt was melting. The stench and mold from the bottom of the basement and its darkness made me so sick that I barely managed not to throw up. I don't know if it's true or not, but I remember somebody telling me that when he was murdering the woman it scared the children into hiding under the bed. They ended up with paint under their nails, forensics said. They had clung to the floor as he tried to drag them out.'

## Track 01: Uncle Evgeni

'I spent that night in the car. In the morning, I went to the spa first, then to the barber. Apparently by that point, the woman's relatives were looking for me. They had been to my house and hadn't found me, so returned to the Unit claiming that everything was Evgeni's fault.

'They wanted to kill me. They had entered the building and vandalised the place. The officer had called the head of the department saying that people had ambushed the building, looting and causing a commotion. When I came back the officer told me to go upstairs because they were waiting for me.

"Who is waiting?" I asked.

"They are here."

'Apparently everyone knew that Kainidze had lost his wife to me in a game of cards and that's why the murder had taken place. How was I supposed to defend myself?'

## Track 07: Former Police Officer

'It was a horrible week, unlike any other I can remember. Three days before, the country had fallen apart. While I was moonlighting in the park, someone lopped off an arm from Lenin's statue. What followed was so crazy one would think they had attacked an actual living leader. The Vice Minister came and caused a huge scene. He declared a state of emergency and alerted every police officer and army officer.

They closed the roads and set up checkpoints throughout the city. They were stopping everyone, searching vehicles, having police dogs run around everywhere, but they could find neither the culprit nor Lenin's broken arm. All he'd done was taken the arm of that cursed man! It made the Vice Minister lose his mind. Instead of finding the culprit, the Ministry brought in a sculptor to make a new arm for the statue. They were afraid that if people saw a statue of an armless Lenin, the word would spread. The sculptor was unsuccessful, the new arm didn't fit properly with the rest of the body, which made the Vice Minister even crazier. After three days, he stormed back into our department shouting, by which point the relatives of the woman had congregated at the front of the building and started throwing stones at it. For once, I was actually glad to see the Vice Minister. Not long before I had been serving in the Uzbekistan military, and had witnessed the lootings in Ferangi. I had seen insane faces before, veins popping, eyes bulging, flushed with blood and drooling… A similar mob was now looking to overrun our building but when they saw the Vice Minister arrive, they evidently calmed down and retreated. They must have thought it meant that Ministry were showing their concern, that they felt their pain. Slowly the protestors began to leave. Only the very close relatives of the unfortunate woman stayed. They weren't sure what had happened and still clung to a hope. I didn't believe what they said about Evgeni. No, I'm not saying he was an angel, but what they were accusing him of was too much. I heard a rumour that before he started working for the Investigations Unit he'd been a street thug, and that he had also been a racketeer on the railroad. But who can say if any of that was true? Everyone who worked with him had a lot of respect for him. He wasn't like the other bosses. He wasn't trying to hide behind anyone; he was willing to take a bullet. I saw that with my own eyes.'

## Track 01: Uncle Evgeni

'As soon as I walked in the Vice Minister brought out his pistol and started screaming blue murder at me. He had on a trench coat and was holding a top hat; he was dressed like a professor. He repeated himself again and again: "Hand over your gun you bastard!" Making sure I was stood in the corner of the room, with no one behind me, I took out my gun and pointed it at his mouth. He backed down and said, "If you're clean, why are you covering for the murderer?" I told him why, but he didn't believe me. He threatened me and asked me again to hand over my gun. I told him to shove it up his ass and threw my gun out the window.

'Then the forensics came back with the results from the bodies, they had reached a verdict and congratulated me on solving the case. They no longer asked about any connection I had with the man or the woman, they didn't even ask me to come to the court. Everything was done and dusted, but I couldn't escape this sense that these events had poisoned my life. Once, years later, when we were still all living together and my wife was still alive, my eldest daughter asked me: "Dad, were you really having an affair with the murdered woman? Did you really win her in a game of cards?"

'I got upset. "Who told you that!" I yelled. She started crying and told me that that's what the girls were saying. I thought I was going to lose my mind. It's why my family fell apart. Then I retired, I was fed up with everything anyhow. I worked for 28 years at the Investigations Unit.'

*

'That was it!' he declared and took another sip from his beer. 'I can't remember everyone's names and last names, but if you are really interested it's all written down in the archive. You can go and see everything.'

'Can I ask you one question?' Redhead interrupted. 'You

really don't know how to play cards?'

Uncle Evgeni reached towards the ashtray, but Baldy beat him to it. 'It filled up so quickly. Let me throw it away.'

★

'*Former Police Officer's Memoir...* That's not a title! That's an example of what a title *shouldn't* be,' the editor-in-chief bellowed. 'It's awful! A headline is supposed to grab the reader, tell them where it's taking them, and shout: *Read me! Quick!*'

Redhead looked worried.

'*Former Police Officer Opens Up About Horrific Murder.* A murder that caused uproar in Soviet Union! Why was this young woman really murdered? Unfounded suspicion, or a life lost in a game of poker?' The anxious news editor was dictating to a woman typing at incredible speed, the words pouring out across a flickering computer screen. He put his papers to one side and looked over at Redhead. Then he took out a match, relit a half-smoked cigarette he took from the ashtray, and let out a long trail of smoke towards the ceiling. The news editor scratched his hairy neck with his index finger. He took one of the pages from the pile on the table and said, 'Didn't I teach you about writing with passion?'

This was on Saturday evening. By Monday morning the newspaper had been printed, running with a front-page story: 'A Life Lost in a Game of Cards!' That was the headline; under it was a standfirst: 'Former police officer's sensational confession.'

The Monday edition sold many copies. Amongst its readers was Uncle Evgeni who concluded that God must be punishing him for his sins.

'When did I say that! I said nothing of the sort!' The former police officer tried to call Redhead and Baldy numerous times. 'You know I never said that. Where did you come up with this? You recorded everything, how could you come up with this?'

★

As always it was dark in the corridor and it smelled of smoke. Whenever they heard footsteps coming down it, the journalists would poke their heads up to look through the glass, hoping it might be the accountant with their pay slips. But this time it was Redhead, so they slouched back to work, unimpressed. At the end of the corridor, he knocked on the door.

'Yes?' came the voice from the inside. When the door opened he was suddenly struck. In a flash of instinct, he covered his eyes as if he'd seen a naked person.

'What's going on?' the editor-in-chief asked. Redhead lowered his hands and looked at the man sitting on the leather couch. The news editor had shaved his beard, which made his face look unnaturally pale, with a distinct tan line, like the ones you see on the bums of boys and girls who've been playing too long in the sun.

'I shaved' the news editor smiled and stroked his pale jaw. 'Did you see the reactions? It's great!'

★

Uncle Evgeni's body was discovered two or three days later. When he hadn't been seen for a few days, Baldy knocked down his door. He was sitting in front of the television with his wig on and his pointy moccasins. His body was moved to the morgue. Baldy was asked to come and identify it formally and sign some papers. The prosecutor uncovered the body and let Baldy see it, naked. 'That's him,' Baldy said, thinking *I killed him*.

'There is no rush, take a closer look,' the prosecutor said.

He looked more closely. It was definitely him, only his skin looked even whiter than usual and, because of this, his faded tattoos stood out more.

'What's that on his shoulder?' he murmured so that the prosecutor would hear too.

'It's a tattoo,' the prosecutor said. 'We made a note of it. Three cards. Aces. With some words written across them:

*Divere est Ludere.*[2] I'm not sure what it means, I will look it up on the internet later. Do you know what it means?'

Baldy didn't know what it meant, and he knew his priest wouldn't allow him to check a foreign dictionary. Not now that the fast had started...

## Notes

1. Named after Jaba Ioseliani, a Georgian politician, 'thief-in-law', and leader of the paramilitary Mkhedrioni organisation, who, shortly after being sentenced to 11 years for banditry, terrorism, and conspiring to kill the president, was granted an official pardon, as part of a general amnesty for convicts, even those convicted for murder.
2. Latin: *Life is a Game.*

# On Facebook

## Gela Chkvanava

### Translated by Tamar Japaridze

ON THE ASPHALT LAID in the courtyard of the tall apartment building during the pre-election campaign, someone had left an inscription in yellow chalk: *ANZOR + THEA = LOVE*. The old-fashioned male name 'Anzor', as well as the word 'love' used instead of the more on-trend heart symbol (which even prevailed in political advertising), gave a comic tint to its content. The heart ideogram itself (with an arrow akin to a spear) had also been added, for good measure, right where Mr Guram, the chemist's Jeep was usually parked.

Mr Guram had taken his son to a relative's wedding in their village that weekend, leaving his wife (who suffered from severe migraines and scarcely ever went out) behind. The night before, someone had stolen the spare tyre from his car. On discovering the theft, he hit the roof and proceeded to whip the city police into a frenzy. But the thief couldn't be found. He had to buy a new spare (for how could he hit the long road without one?).

The local journalist Thea Tetradze was pretty sure that the author of the inscription must have been a student (a freshman, most likely), who had recently arrived from the countryside.

On that gloomy autumn day in Tbilisi, the homeowners that lived in the apartment building began involuntarily calling to mind all the 'Theas' living in their nine-storey building, and concluded there were all too few.

The potential addressees of the inscription could be narrowed down to just three possible candidates:

1. Thea (also known as 'Tiko') Dolaberidze, a medical student aged 19 – the tall daughter of the famous basketball-player Vaso – who wasn't short of her own admirers (although they were usually shorter than her, which got on her nerves);
2. Thea (known as 'Teush' on Facebook) Asatiani, aged 20 – also a university student and a dancer, who often went on tours abroad with her company and brought back a myriad of new shoes and handbags ('that flooded the whole flat,' as her mother would often say). She, too, had a lot of admirers;
3. Tekla Ukleba (registered as 'Teo-Teo' on Facebook), aged 17 – a final-year student at school, who was going to continue her studies at the College of Foreign Languages. (She was a shy, bespectacled girl, so the neighbours barely took her into account.)

There was also Thea Tsuleiskiri, a refugee from Sokhumi – a woman well over 40, who had a fiancé (owner of a small business), who frequently called on his future wife on rainy days with a box of her mother's favourite liqueur-filled chocolates, and fresh editions of *The Whereabouts* and *The Looking-Glass*.[1] (Thea Tetradze, the journalist, had once worked as a sub-editor at the latter).

Those who were eager to identify the addressee of the inscription (i.e. the entire population of the nine-storey building) might have been right when they also failed to take into account Thea Chanadiri. This 'Thea' had divorced her husband three years earlier, and for the time being was a single mother bringing up a six-year-old boy, Gera – named after her former father-in-law. (Gera was set to start school that same year and could yet neither read nor write properly.) Everyone still remembered the passionate story of Thea Chanadiri and her then future (now, unfortunately, ex-) husband, who would roar into the courtyard on his motorbike each day at lightning speed, just to impress her, kicking up a dust-storm that ruined the washing hanging out of the ground-floor windows. (This was during the pre-election campaign period also, and no previous government had cared about repairing skid-marked pavements). All the male occupants of the building swore that when they caught him they'd beat him to death, but none of them could get hold of him.

As for journalist-Thea, she was married. She had frequent rows with her husband (she was in a huff with him on that day too), and regularly turfed him out, only to later let him back in again. On his return, he would always, as a rule, forget to bring the small change needed for the lift service. So, on top of all the other shouting, his wife had to throw coins down at him from the balcony.

As it was a Sunday morning, and nobody had anything particular to do after breakfast, everyone (who could, of course) logged on to their computers and searched for the Facebook profiles of the three above-mentioned candidates, hoping to find an 'Anzor' among their Facebook friends. Journalist-Thea was especially curious, as the mystery stoked the fire of investigative reporting still smouldering within her.

The respectable spouse of Guram the chemist, Tsiala, recalled that in her husband's pharmacy there used to work a young shop-assistant, Lia, who was always dressing provocatively. Several days earlier, Tsiala had found a pack of cigarettes in her husband's car – the same brand that vulgar bitch, Lia, had smoked. Lia (who was from the same part of western Georgia her husband came from) had quit her job six months before, rented a comfortable flat, downtown, and, according to rumour, lived the high life without any income at all. These events had strangely coincided with a period of diminished income at the pharmacy, and things had not recovered (if Guram was to be believed) since.

Someone might have ascribed this jealousy to her goiter, but we must here admit that any woman (even with a healthy thyroid gland) in poor Tsiala's shoes would have been jealous. Tsiala had never forgotten Lia, but this time she had come to mind because her successor (a far more modest girl, by the way) was named Thea. Tsiala also noticed that her husband had lately become an active user of Facebook. She herself was a bit of an old-fashioned woman, and had only previously used the social network site Classmates.com (and only then with the assistance of her son). In other words, she was not on first-name terms with the internet. She decided to ask Dali, her next-door neighbour, for help.

It was ten in the morning, when Tsiala (with a bar of chocolate in her hand) paid Dali a visit. Dali (who was a teacher by profession) had made friends with Mrs Guram because she had helped her to get the medicines for her sick mother at a considerable discount.

'My son Gio has been very sad for a week already. It seems he is in love,' Tsiala told the hostess while sipping her coffee. 'I thought you might help me search his Facebook activity; perhaps we will come across the name of the girl. I don't want him to be snared by some unworthy woman, you know. He is so very young and inexperienced, my sweet boy.'

Dali was planning on searching Facebook that morning anyway, for more information about the three suspects, so she accepted her guest's proposal with pleasure.

Thea Chanadiri was the last among her namesakes to notice the inscription. On reading it, she let out a heavy sigh; her poor soul was thoroughly exhausted by the solitude of being a single mum. A widowed owner of a stationery shop had been making romantic overtures towards her for the last four months. His newly-opened shop was on the opposite side of the street to the office where Thea worked as a manager. The stationer (whom she secretly named 'the Mountain Bear') was a tall, portly man with a tender heart and excellent manners. Every time she saw him, she had a strange sensation that she had known him for a long time; and it is common knowledge that such sensations occurs when a woman has genuine interest in a man.

A week earlier, the Mountain Bear had sent Thea a 'friend request'. The following day he seemed a bit embarrassed when he gave her a plaster piggy bank for her little son. Thea, too, was somewhat confused, and her heart beat a little faster on receiving the present. The boy already had a piggy bank, but Thea was so eager to replace it with her admirer's gift she broke it (as if by chance, of course) while dusting the boy's desk.

Thea was well aware that the Mountain Bear was dying to invite her to the cinema or theatre to establish a closer relationship with her. Well, she wasn't against it, of course, but Achiko was spoiling everything. (Achiko was Thea's line-manager and the cousin of the director's wife). He had great, strong teeth and would flash them every now and then in a Hollywood smile. Achiko was convinced that if he wore tight jeans and smoked expensive cigarettes, every woman would fall for him. And as Thea was divorced, he thought she might be the easiest prey. He always wrote lewd comments under her posts and behaved pretty indecently in the presence of other employees, pretending that Thea was already *his*. Choosing such a strategy (with a little help from his best friend, Koka), he planned to scare away any admirers, and eventually force her into surrender.

That very morning, a new 'surprise' was awaiting poor Thea on her Facebook page: Achiko had sent her a photo by a famous photographer in which a boy, wearing shorts and holding a huge bouquet of roses, was being instructed to deliver the flowers to some lady on behalf of her admirer.

'Idiot!' Thea gasped, her face turning as gloomy as the autumn morning. But a second later, a smile beamed from her face as she noticed another photo (sent a bit earlier by the stationer) depicting an enamoured couple in a boat full of flowers, floating peacefully in the sea. A public declaration of love, she thought!

Thea got so excited she jumped up from her chair.

'It's evidently my day!' she thought and realised that she had been looking forward to this declaration even more impatiently than she imagined. Overwhelmed with happiness, she guessed that the stationer was probably waiting for a comment.

*On what little things does happiness depend!* – she typed rapidly and hit the 'enter' key.

It meant 'I love you too!'

Imagining the stationer's beaming face on reading her comment, she couldn't help smiling.

The Mountain Bear 'liked' Thea's comment instantly and added his own: *It truly does!* (Despite being 15 years her senior and having a strange hobby of making plaster piggy banks of different sizes and shapes, putting photos of them on Facebook pages, and selling them in his shop, he behaved like a little kid every time he came into contact with Thea.)

Naturally, Thea Chanadiri believed in all of the above sentiments, reconciling them with her own experience.

But at that very moment, her notifications icon lit up, indicating that another user – Achiko – had also 'liked' her comment.

A minute later, there appeared a new post on her profile with three smiley stickers: *I'm going to be in your neighbourhood on business; will you offer me a cup of coffee if I call round?*

'This ass-cock (she meant Achiko) is going to scare away any real interest (Mountain Bear)! May the Lord send down on him confusion, rebukes and curses in all he sets his hand to do!' she exclaimed in outrage.

Thea Tsuleiskiri didn't care about the inscription made in yellow chalk outside. She was more concerned with her future sister-in-law's rather ambiguous comment on the photo she'd posted the previous evening. It was a photo of a smiling couple (Thea and her fiancé), and the comment read as follows: *The older my brother gets, the more he takes after our late father in all respects!*

The thing was that her potential sister-in-law didn't approve of Thea Tsuleiskiri from the get-go, and revealed this antipathy at their first meeting by admitting that their father had gone through two previous wives before he met his real better half – their mother. Saying so, she hinted at the possibility of their drifting apart once her brother found a genuine match.

Thea took the hint seriously and began to look on the man she adored with suspicion. It seemed to her that he didn't actually love her, and that he would walk out on her as soon as he got tired of her (as his father had done with his first two spouses).

Having revealed her initial antipathy, the potential sister-in-law started visiting Thea's page from time to time, approving of her posts with 'likes'. Thea took this for a sort of apology, which inadvertently gave the upper hand to her cunning opponent, who in turn took this as the perfect opportunity for launching her coup de grâce.

'I'm a woman of "Balzac Age",' Thea comforted herself and smiled stiffly.

When she was already over 30, before getting acquainted with her fiancé, she used to regularly reassure herself with the same phrase (as though being of 'Balzac Age' added some extra charm to a woman); indeed, it usually helped her in some way, but not this time.

*Right you are, my dear, genes can predetermine everything: a person's appearance, his character and his behaviour!* she commented back to the wicked witch with a sophisticated statement, and spent a good half hour on writing a long email to her fiancé.

The email said that he could stop bringing chocolates and printed matter for her mother; Thea realised now that she had been deceiving both him and herself when she pretended to love him. True, she had succeeded in dazzling him for a time, but she could do nothing with herself. She also confessed that, in the past, she had similarly deceived two other respectable men, and both affairs had ended the same way. She seemed to be destined to only ever truly love one man, who had died long ago. In the end, she asked him to neither answer this email nor try to maintain contact with her in any other way, though she knew he wouldn't. He was a proud man and would never stoop so low as to pursue her after such a rejection. Ending the note with the words, *No one in this life ever gets what they truly want, and everything good comes to an end sooner or later*, she was pleased with how convincing she sounded – especially in the part about the two affairs and the eternal love for the man in the grave. So she added a postscript: *I'm sure, you'll marry a better woman than me, and, despite your genes, you won't need to go through two wives first.* She also mentioned her 'Balzac Age', but then changed her mind and deleted that bit.

As soon as she sent the email, she switched off her telephone and computer, and prepared to read the one-volume edition of Vazha Pshavela's[2] *Poems* (someone had told her that this great man's poetry had once helped Alain Delon through a severe depression, which was approval enough for her). True enough, the poetry gradually eased her out of her dark mood, and she felt grateful to Monsieur Delon, with whom she'd been in love for as long as she remembered.

Thea, the journalist, shared the morning news on her Facebook wall:

*You wouldn't notice anything unusual about our apartment building, just by looking at it, but I can feel it buzzing and humming like a beehive (it's a pity I never made friends with my namesake neighbours and the other Theas in the neighbourhood!). Mark Zuckerberg must have been right when (unlike the designers of Classmates.com), he chose not to install in the Facebook architecture a way of indicating the number of the visitors and searches each profile gets. If he had, I, and five other namesakes, would have gone mad on this morning – the morning His Majesty Commotion and Her Honour Intrigue came to visit, thanks to the inscription in yellow chalk! (Incidentally, he should've used the red chalk piece instead; it would've been more eye-catching!)*

*I appeal to you all to follow suit, and leave your own anonymous inscriptions in your yards to baffle your neighbours! It would also be fun to use the most popular male and female names.* Then she added: *If using the word 'love' makes you uncomfortable, you can always draw a big heart instead!*

*As for my neighbours (young and old), they are still looking for the Anzor (there are only two men with this name in our building, and both are over 50). They are looking for him not only among the Facebook friends of all six Theas (including Chanadiri, Tsuleiskiri, and me) but also among the friends of our friends.*

*In short, it's real bedlam over here, and if the much sought-after Anzor isn't discovered soon, all the husbands of the building's Anzor-hunters will risk going without dinner; their wives don't even have time to watch their Turkish soap-operas, let alone venture into the kitchen!* concluded the restless and loquacious journalist Thea, who didn't think twice about the fate of her three young namesake neighbours.

Thea Dolaberidze's situation was the worst for she had a strict father and an even worse brother (also a basketball-player). The poor girl swore that she didn't know anyone by the name Anzor, and she hadn't given anyone any reason to inscribe her name on the asphalt.

Thea Asatiani's parents decided to investigate the case by first accusing, and then cross-examining their poor girl over the telephone till her credit ran out. This Thea had left her roaming service on when she left for Europe, and hadn't had a chance to top her credit up yet.

Tekla Ukleba was also scolded by her parents and her elder sister (in lieu of a brother). At first, her family didn't suspect her, but when they interrogated her – just to be on the safe side – she blushed, which gave them grounds for suspicion.

The real reason Tekla had blushed was she had had a strange dream the night before. In it, she had been walking with the son of her English teacher (with whom she was hopelessly in love) on the beach of some fashionable resort, leaving wet footprints in the sand (like a couple in some romantic movie). They were both speaking perfect English, without even a Georgian accent. The boy was carrying Tekla's shoes, while Tekla was gathering the fragrant flowers of a Magnolia tree that had washed ashore, then giving them to the teacher's son who would later make a wonderful bouquet.

She woke early the next morning and, charged with the sweet fragrance of the dream, ran to her computer to search for websites that explained dream imagery (websites she was in habit of visiting regularly). When she read about the symbolism of the sea and the flowers, not to mention the meaning wrapped up in the carrying of shoes (her sweetheart also carried his own sneakers, hanging round his neck, their shoelaces tied together), she nearly died with joy.

The inscription left on the asphalt rose, as a topic, higher and higher up the Facebook agenda that day. A resident living on the seventh floor was the first to post a photo of it, taken from his flat window, and kick-started a little competition to see who could take the best quality photo, from every imaginable camera angle.

Another neighbour, living in a one-room apartment, expressed the indignation of his fellows by posting a rebuke to the damned architects of the building who had designed it such that all the one-room apartments faced the street, not the courtyard, thus depriving their owners of the right to observe the inscription from their windows.

God knows how many neighbours became Facebook friends that morning (including many who'd never even said 'hello' to each other before).

As a practical joke, one person wrote that he knew, with complete certainty, the identity of the addressee and the addresser. He immediately received thousands of friend requests and private messages, in which people begged him to reveal the secret and swore it would stay just between them. When in the end he confessed that he knew nothing, he was nearly ostracised.

Facebook users were recalling the minutest details of all the other inscriptions that had ever appeared in the yard, or anywhere else in the neighbourhood; women were sharing memories of how their own husbands first declared their love to them.

The person who had joked about knowing the true identities, declared that it was actually not a joke, and that he really did know who they were. At first, nobody believed him, but soon enough, he was bombarded with the questions again, and didn't dare confess the truth again for quite a while afterwards.

The son of the chemist Mr Guram came to know about the inscription at the wedding reception (reading about it on his mobile), and told all to his father. Mr Guram, the chemist, reacted violently to the news, instantly calling the district police inspector (the same person he had charged with tracking down his stolen tyre), insisting that there must be some link between that theft and the appearance of the inscription the following day. He didn't relent until the inspector promised to personally investigate the matter immediately.

Inspector Berdia Arabuli would never normally agree to such nonsense, but the elections were approaching, and the inspectors were instructed to meet all the demands of the constituents. (The new government had to be careful not to provoke their predecessors, who were now the opposition, of course).

Everybody learned about the inspector's forthcoming visit via Facebook. (The news was spread by the practical joker, so they didn't believe it at first).

On passing his eagle-eyes over the building, the inspector couldn't quite believe what he saw – there was at least one face gazing down on him from every window. Shuddering at the sight, he removed his hat and rubbed his eyes. When some of the homeowners started taking photos of him with their mobiles, he became positively disturbed. He started to suspect the whole thing was a provocation and began to sweat. As a father of three, he was always terrified of being sacked. The poor man looked up at the leaden sky, as if waiting for some sensible explanation of this strange behaviour from above.

This time, Facebook was flooded with the photos of the inspector standing, frozen in panic, beside the inscription in the yard. The building's homeowners were so excited they needed no further prompting from the journalist-Thea. She stopped interfering (the fire of intrigue was already blazing anyway) and simply monitored the many posts and comments of her newly-befriended neighbours. Before long the inscription, as a topic, was forgotten, as various other debates and discussions took precedence; some users even took it as a moment to member departed friends (starting with one of their residents, called Anzor, who had died in a car accident several years before), and confessed that they were all missing them.

Tekla Ukleba, inspired by the occasion, decided finally, after a year's hesitation, to send a friend request to her teacher's son. Yes, it was belated, but he still accepted her.

Journalist-Thea realised that she was out of cigarettes, but she couldn't wrench herself from her computer (despite having switched it to standby), and was beginning to crave them.

In the afternoon it started to rain, and the homeowners unanimously rushed to the windows afraid that the inscription would be washed away (they treasured it now as a symbol of their own collective awakening). *Don't be scared, friends! The inscription won't be as vivid as it is now, but it won't disappear. Remember playing hopscotch as kids? The rain could never completely wash away those chalk squares*, the joker tried to reassure people. This time, they believed him, since they all remembered. But one sceptic still noted back then the chalk was better quality.

*It's a pity the children don't play hopscotch anymore*, someone who 'liked' the sceptic's comment added. *It was still in fashion when we first moved into the building* (i.e. 33 years earlier), another admitted. Then they all started reminiscing about the games they played as children in Tbilisi courtyards. *In old houses with courtyards they still play backgammon and dominos*, someone presented a new theme for discussion, *they even play card games and swear like sailors! There are special pavilions in those older courtyards with long iron tables, benches and a water tap, where people can come together and hold collective feasts! Why can't we do the same?* There instantly came an answer to this last question: *Because people in high-rises like to walk tall, and turn their noses up at the others, even though we all like to boast that we're real townspeople, hailing from the old Tbilisi yard traditions!*

*Not all of us!* commented a third. *Many are from the countryside or provincial cities.* This brought forth a new comment, meant to be a joke and not entirely offensive: *Unfortunately, those provincial newcomers have flooded our beautiful city!* (The author of this joke was not the previous 'joker' but someone else). *What are you saying! Country folk are the best!* this fifth person was offended all the same.

It became apparent that the homeowners of the nine-storey building were now likely to split into hostile factions, according to their social backgrounds. So the journalist-Thea tried to deflate the situation. She posted a photo of her garage taken hastily from her balcony with the comment: *This is my garage, and it's empty (I can't afford a car, anyway). So why don't we use it as our gathering spot and play a game of shinny, backgammon or dominos, sharing our first beer of the day?*

Some of the neighbours liked the idea, and one of them even suggested using *his* garage which had a fireplace they could use for BBQs. But the original joker suddenly remembered that he had neither a garage nor a place to park his car, and admitted: *It's unfair that some homeowners have garages while others don't!* Those in the same predicament rallied to his cause, adding that everything in the yard seemed to depend on your ability to out-do your neighbour. So the situation became tense again.

*Nothing good will come of dealing with the people like you! I'm washing my hands with this, do as you wish!* Thea the journalist was getting angry and decided to go to the shop to get her cigarettes. But alas! She couldn't pull herself from the screen.

*Do any of you realise that the history of our apartment building is being written on Facebook right now?! There is no place for animosity here, even if we have so many bad things to say to one another...* The joker (who was always ready to add fuel to the fire) protested.

Inspector Berdia Arabuli only got to check his Facebook account later that night, and to his surprise discovered multiple friend requests from the homeowners of the apartment building. Consequently he was up till dawn scrolling through everyone's profiles. In the meantime, many interesting events took place:

Thea Tsuleiskiri had been sent a huge bouquet of flowers by her fiancé to make up with her. The bouquet was brought by the Kurd brothers (Thea couldn't see them coming into the yard as she lived in a one-room apartment). The brothers could often be seen begging not far from the building, near the metro station. The younger brother was holding the bouquet solemnly in his hand, escorted by the older one. (As there were two of them, they took turns with the carrying duties, each time they brought one). The homeowners took photos of them too (from different camera angles), and immediately posted them.

About half an hour later, the fiancé's car drove into the yard and took Thea Tsuleiskiri away. The residents immediately started spreading photos of this event among the one-room homeowners, speculating that perhaps the fiancé was apologising for his devil of a sister, taking Thea to some expensive restaurant for a late dinner or early supper. Some even admitted that Thea was 'dressed to kill', though others, who didn't think so, preferred to stay silent.

Strangely enough, by this point, Mrs Guram had learned how to use Facebook thanks to neighbour Dali, and even created her own account. On returning home, she searched for her husband's profile (she couldn't do it in Dali's presence, of course), and to her great surprise, found that the former shop-assistant, Lia, was not among her husband's many Facebook friends, but there was her neighbour Dali among them (Dali was divorced, by the way), and Mr Guram often 'liked' her photos. She also discovered a photo of Dali in a low-cut dress that her husband had commented on in Latin: *Mens sana in corpora sano*,[3] which Dali 'liked', and put a lot of smiley stickers under, by way of a comment on his comment.

Yeah, life didn't give that woman many breaks. Poor Tsiala!

Thea, the journalist, was certainly joking when she announced that she was going to create a specially dedicated Facebook group called 'Neighbours'. She posted a photo of their apartment building cut-and-pasted from Google Street View which she suggested could be the profile pic, and encouraged people to support the idea. Later, she pushed the idea even further and suggested to start an entirely new social media platform here in the building, as Zuckerberg had done it when he first weaved his cobweb for his fellow students. Was that rich college boy any better than her? No way!

The idea she'd had earlier - encouraging friends to make similar inscriptions in their yards - started to give Thea Chanadiri another idea: a trick to play on her annoying admirer Achiko that would ruin him thoroughly.

First of all, she opened a Word file and wrote, *ACHIKO + KOKA =,* then expanded the text to the largest possible font size, and printed out each character on a separate sheet of paper. Then she carefully cut these letters out with tiny scissors in order to make stencils from the remaining paper (with a pencil she drew a rose, thinking it more impressive than a heart symbol, and did the same). When it stopped raining, she bought a spray can from the nearest hardware shop and gave it, along with the rest of her spare cash and the stencils, to the older of the Kurd brothers standing at the traffic lights. She told him that she had decided to play a trick on her close friends. The Kurdish boy was happy to spray the above-mentioned text on the cement wall in front of Achiko's house after dark for 27 laris. (There was much more money in the piggy bank, but the spray can wasn't cheap.) The boy couldn't read or write any Georgian, so Thea numbered the letters and even scribbled a cheat sheet on his dirty palm.

It wasn't difficult to find Achiko's newly-built high-rise in the old district of the city (Thea had found it on Google Street View in seconds, and even scrutinised the cement wall in front of it in depth).

By the evening, Thea the journalist had calculated that there was only one Thea to every nine homeowners in their building, while the ratio between certain other names and the homeowners was 2.5 times higher. So she declared that all Tinatins[4] needed to be taken a special care of. *They should be listed as endangered species*, the joker joked (he must have been very tired, as his jokes were growing increasingly insipid), and added a new post: *If anyone is going out for cigarettes, please buy a pack for me too. I'll give you the money - for the lift service too - right at the door of the lift.* There appeared to be more than one late-night cigarette buyer willing to help. All refused to take the lift money, so Thea the journalist invited them for a cup of tea, asking them to bring some sugar too, as she'd run out of that as well. The newly-befriended neighbours willingly accepted her offer.

When it got dark, the sky cleared and there appeared twinkling stars and a crescent moon in the sky.

Thea Chanadiri, who had long wanted to teach Achiko a good lesson, felt a pang of conscience at the thought of his neighbours mocking him for being gay; she also regretted that she had broken her son's original piggy bank. That said, she'd already justified the act with the thought that the inscription would help Achiko's neighbours come together as a community. Then her inbox pinged red with a private message from the Mountain Bear, observing that a stupid inscription seemed to have caused mayhem among Thea's neighbours. *The Thea mentioned in it is not me*, Chanadiri replied. *Besides, nobody is in the habit of visiting me for a cup of coffee*, she added. *I know*, came the answer. *I was afraid you didn't*, Thea wrote back. *I would never think that*, the Mountain Bear confirmed again, and invited her to a café the following day. Thea preferred going to the cinema, but she understood that the café suggestion was a consequence of her earlier coffee comment. *On what little things does happiness depend!* she posted before going to bed.

Overtired and worried Tekla Ukleba fell asleep as soon as the moon climbed into the sky. She was smiling in her sleep, maybe even dreaming a sweet dream in English.

At that moment Thea (Teush) Asatiani was admiring her two new bags (bought to spite her parents) in a hotel room somewhere in Europe.

As for Thea (Tiko) Dolaberidze, she had decided to get married and escape her unforgiving father and brother as soon as possible. But when she checked the list of her admirers, her heart sank – all those who were tall enough seemed far too dull, and she would never agree to marry a man shorter than her. So she locked herself in her room and cried bitterly, repeating the well-worn adage about God having nothing to do with the business of creating woman.

Thea Tsuleiskiri had enriched Facebook with a new group called 'Atinati'. Any Tinatin (with any variation of the name) could become a member. The first to 'like' her page was her future sister-in-law.

*God bless the limitless power of Facebook!* Thea the journalist posted before going to bed (once again comparing her apartment block to a buzzing beehive). *Till tomorrow, my dear neighbours! Take care, not only of the Theas out there, but also of yourselves and one another!*

P.S.
A week later, right on the Election Day, they learned that a tenant renting a flat in the neighbouring apartment building – a village girl called Thea, who was a first-year student at some university – had been kidnapped by another student who was in love with her. It was evident that the author of the inscription (who must have been drunk while making it) had accidentally mistaken their nine-storey building for his sweetheart's one.

## Notes

1. *The Whereabouts*, *The Looking-Glass* – the newspaper and the magazine noted for sensationalism.
2. A great Georgian poet (1861-1915).
3. A Healthy Mind in a Healthy Body.
4. The full version of Tea, Tiko, etc.

# Precision

## Erekle Deisadze

### Translated by Philip Price

#### 1.

WHEN PEOPLE DIE, THEY get buried. In Tusi's case, it happened the other way around. First they buried her, then she died.

It doesn't matter, in the end, whether they heap sods of earth on you, or wrap you up warm in a woollen blanket – the feeling of suffocation is just the same.

Tusi is my sister. We've been living in a train carriage for the last three-and-a-bit years. The carriage is parked right on the outskirts of the city, but it doesn't take too long to get to the centre if you know the right roads. During the day, Tusi stays at home alone. The little stereo she keeps next to her helps her pass the time. Before she goes to sleep, she asks me to read her a few psalms. I don't know how it helps her, but she says it makes her sleep better.

I spend the first half of the day in the gardens surrounding Kashveti Church, and the second half at the entrance to Rustaveli metro station. In the interim, me and Koka sniff glue and I try to forget about Tusi for a while. Koka is two years younger than me. We met in the toilets at McDonalds, when he ushered me silently into one of the stalls and handed me a polythene bag filled with solvents. Me and Tusi have each other. Koka doesn't have anyone.

My father died in the August War with Russia. After that, I never saw my mother again. The last time I saw my dad was when we went to the morgue to identify him. What I remember most clearly is his burnt flesh. I also remember Tusi screaming during the bombing raid, just before she fell to the ground and lost consciousness. Tusi was 17 then, and I was 14. The glove she always carries around with her used to be my mother's. Now it is Tusi's property.

'See?' she says, shoving the glove under my nose. 'It smells of mum!'

To me it smells of something else entirely.

A year ago, Tusi started to feel unwell. She was examined free of charge as part of a government programme to help people suffering hardship as a result of the war. The diagnosis was harsh.

'She has cancer,' the doctor said.

'No she doesn't,' I replied.

The doctor patted me on the shoulder and showed me out.

That night me and Koka smashed a supermarket window and stole a load of sweets. I wanted them for Tusi, who was waiting for me at home, tired and depressed.

'Where did you get them from?' she asked.

'The priest gave me them.'

'You better not be lying to me.'

'I'm not lying to you.'

'Swear on it then.'

'I swear to God.'

That seemed to calm her down. And anyway, I knew for a fact God wouldn't strike me down just because I swore to him when I was telling a lie.

'Have you been for the test results?' she asked me.

'Yeah.'

'What did they say? How long have I got?'

'It's all going to be alright, thank God,' I said, swallowing hard as I ran outside. I didn't want her to see me crying. I had to read a lot of psalms to Tusi that night before she went to sleep, but eventually she closed her eyes, satisfied.

## 2.

When they shelled our block, Tusi and I were standing in a circle in the courtyard with some other kids and playing with a ball, while the men played dominos. The sound of the explosion made everything shake. I remember seeing white smoke rising up around us, and pieces of shrapnel hitting Tusi, but I don't remember anything after that.

When I opened my eyes, I was in hospital. I had been asleep on one of the wards. I clambered out of bed without anyone noticing me, and staggered out into the corridor. The wounded were pouring into the reception area in an unending stream. I knew no one would notice I was gone, so I started poking my head round the doors of all the wards, searching for Tusi. I found out later that Tusi had undergone a serious operation which had left her permanently crippled. In itself, that wouldn't normally have been enough to stop us picking up our game where we left off – after a certain amount of time, of course – but we just didn't want to any more, and we couldn't anyway. Our desire to play and the possibility of doing so disappeared along with our mother.

I'm standing alone outside the metro station. It's the middle of the day, and the heat is unbearable. I look up and see Koka walking towards me. He is holding a rose in his hand and sniffing it absent-mindedly. He's wearing a stupid hat.

'You need a top-up?'

'Not yet,' I answer curtly.

He sits down next to me. The pause in the conversation goes on so long it starts to feel uncomfortable.

'I've fallen in love,' he says eventually.

'Who with?'
'She works in there,' he says, pointing at McDonalds.
'What's her name?'
'Nino.'
'Does she know?'
'Not yet.'

*It was as hot as it is now on that day too*, I think, staring at an old woman selling balloons.

### 3.

'Someone was here,' said Tusi.

'When?'

'This afternoon.'

'What did they want?'

'He said he was a social worker. He even left a card. He said they're implementing a government programme to help families in great need.'

'Sounds like bullshit,' I said.

'They announced it on the radio as well. I heard it myself.'

Tusi pulled a comb through her hair and raised her head up towards the flickering lightbulb.

'Look. My hair has started to fall out.'

I felt an unbearable pain in my stomach, but I pretended I wasn't listening.

'I'm going to be bald, on top of everything else!' said Tusi, laughing.

'What are you going on about now? You're getting on my nerves.'

I snatched the comb out of her hand and threw it with all my strength out of the open door.

'What did you do that for? You idiot!' said Tusi, sticking out her lower lip.

I hugged her with all my strength, and tried to hold back my tears with all my strength.

'Maybe this is how it's meant to be,' said Tusi quietly, patting my back with her skinny hand.

Around dawn I was woken by Tusi muttering in her sleep. She was mumbling bits of the psalms. Her face was white as a cloud. I wiped her dry lips with a lemon and took her temperature. 39.6 degrees.

### 4.

Early the next morning, as Tusi slept peacefully, I saw someone's face appear out of nowhere through the curtain covering the window of our carriage. Then I heard a loud knocking sound. A well-built man was standing in the doorway, holding a form in one hand and gesturing to me politely with the other.

'I'm Melori,' said the visitor.

'Pleased to meet you,' I replied.

'I've already been here once, but you weren't at home. I'd like to talk to you.'

'About what?'

'I think that much is clear,' said the visitor, clearly offended. 'It is my job to help you. It goes without saying, of course, that the state would never deprive one of its citizens of palliative care. Furthermore, you have the status of officially displaced persons, which means there is a good chance you are entitled to a fixed amount of monthly financial assistance. In addition, please don't worry about your sister's first course of chemotherapy – the costs of that have also been covered by the state.'

### 5.

'How about we put her on here?' I asked in a tired voice, and with the help of the visitor pulled out the bookcase.

'What if she falls off?' he asked doubtfully.

'She won't… I don't think,' I replied, brushing away a cobweb stretched between the bookcase and the wall.

The floor was covered in a thick layer of dust. Two cockroaches scrambled out from their invisible hiding place and set off in a fixed direction. The bulb dangling from the ceiling gave off barely any light, but even in the semi-darkness, the stranger filled in the form like a natural, carrying out his duties with admirable dedication. He had clearly found his calling in life. Every word he uttered and every movement he made had only one aim – to achieve the greatest possible degree of precision.

'Can't you just measure her in hand spans?' I asked.

'Absolutely not,' he replied disparagingly. 'The state demands precision. It is essential that we use a tape measure.'

### 6.

A radio receiver, a lightbulb, three cups, two plates, a bed, a bookcase, a wash rag, a broom, a small aluminium pan, two pairs of shoes, a tablespoon, a knife and a fork; these were the everyday items which the visitor noted on his form. He inspected every one of them in detail, as if trying to discover some new quality to them. He held a neatly sharpened pencil in his chubby fingers, and traced out each letter and numeral with singular precision. He must have been top of his class at school. His clean-shaven face wore a severe expression. The collar of his white shirt peeked out from his checked pullover. Little by little, the musty smell in the room was replaced by the scent of his aftershave. Before long it had spread through the entire carriage.

Then Tusi woke up. She smiled coldly at the visitor and asked me to bring her some water.

'How are you?' asked the visitor politely. 'We've been getting to know each other while you were asleep. You have a splendid little brother.'

'We're looking for the tape measure,' I said.

'I think it's in one of the books,' said Tusi, and then added, after a brief pause, 'I was using it to mark my place.'

'Which book?' I asked.

'Do you like poetry?' asked the visitor for some reason.

'No,' replied Tusi brusquely.

'Which book?' I asked again.

'*The Trial*, I think' said Tusi, yawning. 'I'm pretty sure it's in *The Trial*.'

## 7.

Our trial didn't take too long. We pulled off Tusi's blanket, revealing her threadbare night dress, and through it her white stomach. Confused and embarrassed, she inhaled sharply and glared at me. I put my hand on her wrist and whispered: 'Don't be scared'.

The visitor unrolled the tape measure and took the length of Tusi's left leg first, followed by her right. He held one end of the tape against her knee, and the other on the sole of her foot.

'Well that's a shame,' he said.

'What's wrong?' I asked.

'We're just a few millimetres short.'

I didn't have a clue what he was talking about, so I chose to stay silent. As the visitor wrote the new data on the form, I kissed Tusi on the forehead.

'Tell him to leave soon,' she whispered to me.

'In order to qualify for government assistance, the leg that is to be operated on must be at least five centimetres shorter than the other one,' said the visitor and then added, after a short pause, 'Yours is four centimetres and 95 millimetres.'

'Tell him to go. Please,' said Tusi, covering herself up with the blanket.

'Yes, I'm going. It's really quite heart-rending, though. Just five millimetres,' said the visitor without the slightest trace of emotion. Then he put his face close to mine, flared his nostrils, and whispered: 'The state loves precision'.

'The state loves precision,' I repeated.

The visitor went soon after that. Before he left, I signed the form. I stayed by Tusi's side, not bothering to show him out.

### 8.

Warm summer rain fell that night. The smell of earth wafted up into the carriage. I stood in the open doorway and let the raindrops strike my face. Tusi was sitting on the bed, leaning against the carriage wall and listening to the radio. An ambulance drove past somewhere in the distance, its muffled siren coming closer and then fading away.

'Do you think dead people can tell when it's raining?' she asked me.

'Yeah. Probably,' I answered.

Tusi told me she didn't want me to read any psalms to her before bed. She pulled herself over to one side of the bed and asked me to lie down next to her. Then we fell asleep. Or at least Tusi did. I stayed awake, thinking about the wilting rose she had hidden under her pillow.

### 9.

One month later, Tusi shaved her head. We had loads of arguments about it.

### 10.

We buried Tusi yesterday. The funeral expenses were covered by the state. The district governor came, and even a few TV journalists. Me and Koka stood side by side in front of the open grave, and as a big fuck you to the world, I made sure I didn't cry. Koka didn't cry either – he did himself proud. It was only when they had finished filling in the grave that I noticed a couple of tears making streaks down his unwashed face. A week later they moved me to new accommodation, but without Tusi everything felt empty.

Yesterday I found a little stray puppy by the entrance to the metro station. I took it home and called it Tusi.

Now there are two of us again.

# Peridé

## Zviad Kvaratskhelia

### Translated by Mary Childs

#### 1.

As SOON AS I lift my head from the pillow, I have to pounce at the curtains – I don't want water, I don't even pee or stretch – I jump up, throw back the curtains and all is well. It's like this: every morning I watch as she lowers her head and circles the sports ground endlessly. No matter what the weather, even if it's pouring, or there's slush still on the roads, it's always the same, like a court order, without tiring – go!

In the beginning I was amused, and even counted how many laps she would do. It was a matter of curiosity, how much a woman who'd never been to a sports field in her life before and who's past middle age, is capable of with her slow, even gait. They say eventually a person starts to resemble their profession: if you observe your neighbourhood cobbler closely, well, you'll see that in some ways he looks like the shoes lined up on the table in his tiny booth, as if there were miniature clones of him arranged there, rather than rows of tattered, worn-out things. I could never imagine that this woman, who was used to a sophisticated, highly cultured lifestyle, would ever go near a sports field. Sure, it's understandable that any living being needs exercise and physical activity – when the brain is tired, you need to work your muscles – but why did she choose old age as the time to show off? The women in our neighbourhood are green with envy, their hearts burn with anger, and they pour golden words of gossip into each other's ears about her.

Her name is Peridé. She doesn't talk to anyone, and doesn't pay attention to anyone either. It's a blessing that I remember when she and her husband first moved here more than thirty years ago. Otherwise, I might have believed she was not of this world, and that they'd brought her here from a parallel universe.

At the time, they were allocating apartments, having constructed new buildings on the Nutsubidze Plateau. There was a mad scramble for these new apartments, as they came up so rarely. I was one of them. If you didn't have connections, you could end up suffocating to death in a 'Khrushchyovka' bedsit.[1] Back in the day, the Soviet system would wring every last drop out of you, so you had to make the most of everything and grab any chance you could to live like a human being.

I think the Gugunavas moved here in 1984. Like many other people, they were starting from scratch. When they had their housewarming party they invited only a handful of us. It was a modest affair: they had two children, and lived like church mice. Peridé made a delicious spicy beef stew which she ladled into shallow bowls, then she set a cucumber and tomato salad topped with green onions in the middle of the table, poured wine, and said, 'Excuse me, my students have come; I have to leave you for a while.'

Peridé tutored children in Georgian, and I asked her if my own relatives could join her class a couple of times. At the end of the year, I brought her the cash, but she point-blank refused to take it. 'There's no way,' she said. I shouldn't have been surprised, but I was. We weren't the kind of neighbours who completely depended on each other, but then, I also knew what hell tutoring could be. But she refused, and pushed the envelope containing 25 ruble notes back at me. We were standing by her new iron door as we were having this argument.

## 2.

Did I close the door? Yes, probably. Yes or no? Damn! I remember that I closed the bathroom door and turned the light off. I turned the oven off, too. I was drinking coffee in the kitchen – that's when the alarm clock rang. Yes, that's what happened.

One lap takes two and a half minutes. At first, it's hard, the cold air constricts your lungs, your bones aren't warmed up yet. Your heart pounds, and the wind bites at your face. The apartment blocks are multiplying round here. Soon we'll be in a city of apartment blocks, and they'll get rid of this ministadium, with its white doors and newly-laid artificial turf. No one will raise a peep, because we're all cowards. And in return, we'll all have two bathrooms instead of one, and a car at our beck and call. Central heating, improved living conditions.

On the third lap, I have to speed up, but carefully. The second building now has 40 windows. When I counted them yesterday morning there were 42. Where did those two windows go? These shameless people didn't brick them up, did they? Ah well, it's no big deal, they probably bricked it up and plastered it smooth over night. And, who are you going to complain to anyway, what are you going to say? In 1984, when we moved here, this neighbourhood still looked like something, a place where you could take a child out into your yard, or go for a walk, and the people were different then. You saw more humans than buildings, and you didn't feel like you were alone.

'Tiótia Peridé!'[2] Not a week would pass without that unbearable Kurdish girl Sonia showing up. During the summer, she would sell raspberries; in October, potatoes and feijoas; in winter – dresses. She would insist on giving us credit, so she had a reason to come back next time. My husband and the girls would always be irritated by these appearances and would need calming down. 'Tiótia Peridé, Tiótia Peridé!' I would open the door on her second attempt. I'd bring her into the kitchen; she would take out her goods, and for two whole hours we'd bargain: 'Can you give it to me for three and a half rubles?' *'No, klianus', ne mogu.'*[3] 'Then, I don't want it.' 'OK, so be it.' 'I'm prepared to buy two dresses but only if you lower the price by ten rubles.' 'No, Tiótia Peridé, that's what *I* paid for it.' 'You have to give me a discount.' 'No, no, klianus', that's it. This is not no first, then yes! This is just no, that's it.' Sonia would get mad and pace back and forth across the room. Exhausted from all the teaching, these arguments with the Kurdish girl would bring me back to life. 'Tea or coffee? I have some delicious chocolates.'

My father, may he rest in peace, used to say, 'Eat, before it becomes something you only dream about.' Whenever we started being picky, he wouldn't get mad or raise his voice, he'd just say: 'Eat, before it becomes something you only dream about.' And it was true. You couldn't take things for granted: not just chocolate or treats, but even bread sometimes, often my husband, nearly always my husband, had to stand in a kilometre-long queue for it. We were a nation of queues. A city of queues. We spent our honeymoon in Riga – who remembers when that was! But it was our honeymoon, and good times. They say that as you get older, the sweet memories stay with you. No such thing! Fights, struggling, these are the fragments that stay with you. We stood in queues. Cold, hunger, insomnia, anger – they all came together. You'd talk to someone just because you wanted to remind yourself you were human. It was evening. Or it was early morning, and gradually people would be coming out to join the queue. Before long they were going to explode, you thought. This hell was only missing a single burning log. Then suddenly you'd hear an awful barking and whining. *God, why are you doing this to us!* The line would narrow, burst in the middle, and that horrible woman's horrible dogs would start attacking each other. Not one or two, but ten, or more. 'Sshhhh, sshhhhh, don't be afraid, they won't bite you,' she'd say. And everyone believed her. But not me, I wasn't stupid. I had children. What do you think's gonna happen when you send your kids off to school each morning, carrying their lunches, and a pack of dogs is waiting outside? A pack of hungry, homeless animals. I wanted to drag her by the hair, that embodiment of humanity, but the neighbours held me back. 'Either you take them away, or I'll call the police, and they'll kill them with pleasure.' She was pale and shocked. 'Ma'am, what is your problem with them? They're poor, homeless dogs,' she said. 'I think you don't realise they're dangerous,' I replied. 'At any time, God forbid, they could bite someone, and it won't be a pretty sight.' The woman was shocked and fell silent. She listened tensely as I went on: 'Not by tomorrow, no, not by tomorrow, but by Monday, if I see a single one of them near the building's entrance, I won't be able to answer for my actions.' Others were beginning to agree with me, cheering me on: 'Yeah. That's how it is!' Some of them were quiet, though, not daring to utter a word. Emboldened, I carried on: 'You will do the right thing, and by Monday you'll get rid of these vagrants. That gives you plenty of time. We can wait three more days. A person can survive in the rain for three days. We can stand in line all day for two tiny loaves of bread; we can endure this ridicule, so we can deal with you easily.' 'Yeah, well said, Peridé. You're right!' the others joined in. The women were egging me on: 'To think, a man can't say this to her; but a ballsy woman can!' This is how they supported me, but still, the guilt about those poor dogs stayed with me. Who knows where they were dragged to, or what kind of hellish pit they were thrown into. In my village, when a dog had puppies, they would keep one or two males, and the rest they would tie up in a bag and leave in a field to die. As a child, I felt so sorry for these puppies. I would imagine their suffering, complain to my grandmother, and plead with her: 'When we have puppies, we're not going to put them in a bag, are we?! Please, promise me.' 'No, no, my dear,' she would say. As you get older, the sweet memories stay with you – so they say. Well, here's some 'sweet' memories for you: hard work, constant struggling, people's anger towards you lasting years and years. While some people cheered me on, apparently half the building was reviling me behind my back. 'That mean and ruthless woman, what could she possibly teach children; she can't even tolerate a few stray dogs.' And you call them humans, this two-faced herd with no principles. They can't stand by their word. They change their opinion once a week, like soap. I'm not frightened of them, I thought, and decided never to say hello, or smile, or be friends with any of them, ever again. Even if it meant living alone, having no one to talk to; I didn't want it. It was because of people like that we turned into a city of apartment blocks.

Soon, very soon, this whole sports field will have been swept away... What the hell happened to those windows? Yesterday morning there were 42, and just now when I counted them, there were only 40. They probably bricked it up and plastered it smooth over night. I know how that story goes.

### 3.

Finally, she's stopped. Sometimes, she goes on and on, circling round and round. Sometimes she'll pick up her pace, and I'll hear the rustling of her rain pants from my open window.

Since she's been alone, and her married daughters don't go out of their way to help her, I think she's become more of a loner. The Gugunavas never were big socialisers, but since the day the neighbours got into that fight over the dogs and she clashed with Lira Shavishvili, Peridé has been quiet. No one ever sees her sitting in the yard any more. Evil tongues say she has run out of students, and that she turned down those few teaching hours she was offered at the university the year before last. 'I've grown old; I'm tired. It's not like I'm not going to kill myself,' she says. That remains for others to see – in the morning, a few minutes before seven, she comes out into the sports ground, lowers her head, and circles the field endlessly.

Right now, she is closing the sports ground's iron gate noisily, turning the lock two, three times, and making her way out to the road.

She has to walk past our entrance. I've noticed that she often pauses by my window for a few seconds, exhaling and inhaling deeply. She always looks forward as she does this, never turns her gaze to the side.

It's as if she's following a stopwatch; she snaps out of her momentary torpor, takes two steps, and freezes on the spot as if struck by lightning.

A Chihuahua puppy is standing on the Bokhua's balcony, looking out. It's yapping and bashing itself against the iron railing, trying to find a way out. Sometimes it rears up on its hind legs, sometimes it puts its head through a circle in the railing and growls at the strange woman, barking and trying to get at her. Peridé is standing, startled, confused. But then her tense face opens, softens, and smiles.

The Bokhua's Chihuahua is throwing itself against the railing, its paws skidding on the slippery tiles, before it collides with the balusters. He's yapping and trying to get close to her. Peridé still stands there, too stunned to move. She's looking up at the balcony, and the smile can't be wiped off her face.

4.

'Hello, Miss Lira, I'm Peridé… yes, from the third building. I'd like to talk to you.'

## Notes

1. The unofficial name of a type of low-cost, brick or concrete-panelled apartment building, developed in the Soviet Union during the early 1960s (Nikita Khrushchev's era).
2. Tiótia: Russian for 'Aunt'.
3. Klianus', ne mogu: Russian for 'I swear, I can't'.

# Tsa

## Iva Pezuashvili

### Translated by Mary Childs

#### 1.

BEFORE I LEFT MY house, my underwear ripped, right over my butt. This was a very strange and dangerous moment. I was sitting down in an armchair and heard the sound of fabric ripping. Some kind of irrational fear overcame me; my heart started pounding. I needed two or three seconds to deduce that I faced no danger, or no *further* danger, and that which had just happened had so because I'd gained weight... a lot of weight. And I don't know how this happened. It's been almost a year since I've had a job, and I wander around without money. My aunt supports me and, as her unfortunate dependent, I've gotten used to the taste of cheap food, like borscht with meat, or green beans. To recap, I've gained weight, and now my underwear is ripped right over my butt. What's more, I had to go to a trashy, but popular TV station for a job interview, and because of this underwear, or gaining weight, I was running late. I shouted out to my aunt to bring me some underwear. She was busy making dinner, I think eggplant, or cauliflower, or something. Only a person who was living off his aunt would eat this kind of food...

I had to walk half-naked across the apartment to get my underwear myself. We lived in a traditional Tbilisi courtyard, and to walk in front of the windows was not to be taken lightly. Spying through the windows was one of the favourite amusements of the older neighbours; they stared into the windows facing the yard with such interest and stubbornness that a certain character of Hitchcock's would be envious. In short, you couldn't hide anything from them; if you were going to do something bad it was better to step back from the window first. In a Tbilisi courtyard, the windows are the second enemy of the overweight, bare-arsed man (the first is gravity).

I was about to tread cautiously past the window when I noticed something new and strange down in the courtyard, so strange that my neighbours quite overlooked my nakedness. Three Asian women, compact and not dressed for the season, were striding towards the spiral stairs that stood in the centre of the yard and led to the balcony of my floor. They were followed by some workmen. These guys were dragging in very big, clunky white furniture for the women.

One of the Asians was quite striking: thin, with long, black hair. I looked at her face, and thought I'd never seen such a beautiful girl in all my life. I was surprised to find Asians living so close to me, even more so that they were all women. My neighbours were also staring at these women – they were so happy! Now, they all had something to talk about, and would no doubt make a huge fuss throughout the neighbourhood with this news. Thanks to the sudden appearance of these women, I had forgotten all about my nakedness. The sight of this long-haired girl enchanted me... I felt somehow elated, and I began looking for my underwear more cheerfully.

Eventually, I found them, and left the flat. Running into the workmen on the balcony, I asked them who the women were. This is when I learned they were Chinese.

'They're definitely masseuses,' one of the workmen said, and winked at me.

'You'll have nice, cute masseuses for neighbours,' the other added.

'I don't know about Chinese masseuses,' the first one said. 'But in the olden days the Vietnamese exported these amazing creams for relaxation purposes; you should have seen them – they could cure everything, from pulled muscles to diarrhoea.'

'Could do with them, in our line of work,' said the second worker. 'It's one or the other: either your muscles are torn, or your gut revolts.'

They were a strange pair. I smiled at them and made my way out. But as I walked, I couldn't stop thinking about my new Chinese neighbours. What the hell did they want in this city? I hailed a taxi.

I shared my thoughts with the driver. 'Those folks that our previous President brought here – screw them! The same goes for everyone that guy allowed in – Indians buying land in Kakheti – to hell with them!'

'These ones are Chinese,' I explain.

'It's them or us, I tell you. They'll swallow us whole, if we let them! They fornicate in their massage parlours – I'm not against it, you understand – Chinese whores aren't as bad as some. But you should see the Indian and Iraqi nightclubs in my home town. They're a disgrace. They're taking our Georgianness away from us and they're discriminating against us, not letting us in. They're letting foreigners do it with Georgian women, d'ya get me...?' Then he talked about his religious beliefs, and told me he wouldn't mind visiting these Chinese women. 'They're very tight,' he said through slobbering jowls, 'not as satisfying as Georgian women, though.'

He was a foul-mouthed taxi driver. I'm no angel myself, but I couldn't stand that kind of male conversation. And of course, he didn't have change for a five, so he pocketed an extra *lari*...

Screw it... I lost both underwear and a *lari* today...

I got out of the car and my aunt phoned. She needed basil... She's feeding me such horrible stuff! I can barely swallow it, so why am I gaining weight? After my aunt, the bank called because I hadn't paid my latest installment, and they were now adding an extra percentage point. After I lost my job, I couldn't pay my loan, so every day I'm late on an installment, they add a percentage to the interest. I think I was paying ten times more than the original amount. I didn't know what kind of a horrible offer they were going to make me at this trashy TV station, but I would take it, no matter what. After all, losing my job was my fault. I had stuck to my principles, and because of that I now owed a lot of money.

It had been New Year's Eve. We were all in the office, editing that night's edition. First, they phoned the editor and the journalist, and let them know they were both fired. The editor was over 40, a father of four – can you imagine how shocked he must have been? The journalist was the pampered daughter of a millionaire, with no more than a secondary school education and an artificial physiognomy – injected lips and lifted eyes. She was working just for fun, but she still felt bitter at being fired, probably because it was New Year's Eve, and all of us were expecting a nice bonus or something, not to be fired. We still had to keep at it, the show was to be aired in just a few hours... But a strange feeling came over me. I was both worried about my colleagues, and petrified of them calling me, too. It was natural to be nervous, and I was worried about *looking* worried, but at the same time I wished they'd just get it over with: tie me up and smear me in honey, so at least I'd know which insects were biting me...[1] As it happened, they phoned me a few minutes later and said I was to keep my job because I was a good producer. In fact, they were going to give me a new program, although my salary was to be reduced by three hundred *lari*. Our director's New Year cynicism. I hung up the phone coldly and started to think. The show had to air a couple of hours later, so I asked the journalist and editor to help me finish it. It occurred to me to write a new piece especially for the journalist – a tasty little morsel in the style of the Dada Manifesto – then we waited for 8 o'clock to arrive. We managed to give the program to the broadcasting department at the very last second, so the editors weren't able to go over it, and our Manifesto aired, prime time... And this is how we all wished 'Happy New Year' to our jobs:

'You all need an enema...'[2]

## 2.

A year had passed since this incident, and no TV station would hire me. But now, some new, grand project was being planned by one of the trashy, but very popular channels, and they needed my help as an eccentric producer. And, as I found out over the phone, they were offering me a very good salary, and my line-manager would be a former colleague of mine.

Yes! My new boss was my former co-worker. In my previous job, the locker room talk had it that all the new men in production – the 'televirgins' – would become men with this woman. But now, they all said, she only gives it to the bosses...

On my first day in the new job, she came at me again with the same old litany: she told me I'd gained weight, and that it didn't look good on me; that I smoke too much, and that they were only hiring me because they were amused by the story of my previous rebelliousness, although that kind of thing wasn't going to fly here. She told me they were launching a huge, new show where people would be able to present their talents, or lack thereof. When she told me this, I was genuinely happy. I imagined I would be giving real opportunities to people, but she quickly disburdened me of this delusion. It was not my business to open doors to talent. My task was to find crazy characters who would do any stupid thing just to be famous, just to appear on TV. I was to sit down and trawl through viral videos, and bring internet heroes to the in-house casting department. And if her majesty, my boss, and her fuck-buddy, who was also a member of the jury, decided that this character was crazy enough and gullible enough to do anything, we would get them on the show. We would get them on the show, and people would laugh, and the show would score well in the ratings, and I would get a nice, fat bonus for each hyperactive crackpot I brought in. I listened to her without saying a word, and I couldn't understand why she didn't want me to look for real talent. In spite of the fact that I have very few friends, I still had a wide circle of acquaintances, and I could find some genuine talents. When I shared this, she told me I didn't have to worry about it. Talent would not be lost, and would find its way to casting just as before, but these crackpots wouldn't come forward by themselves. Then she added, 'What do you think? Who's the viewer going to like more, a mediocre singer you can find by the bucketful in this country, or the kind of character that no one has seen yet?' If TV producers weren't allowed to justify their work by using viewers in their defence, they'd never be able to sleep at night. And you, Madame Producer, why would we make such ridiculous shows, where the host literally presides over the rest of us, telling us what to think, or disingenuously shares our sorrows with us, asking idiotic questions? You even had a cartoon character hosting one of your shows! In short, these TV workers have fallen into a great morass, and at the same time they claim that people are watching this morass, that people *need* this morass. People involuntarily watch whatever they're given. What else can they do – watch nothing?

I don't know why I felt disappointed when I left my new boss, after that first meeting. Everything was so familiar and simple. I was doing the same thing as before, wasn't I? The same thing, that is to say nothing meaningful or useful. This life is a very strange compromise. I remembered how, in my previous job, they fired one young man because he was too intellectual. It doesn't matter whether your workplace is in the government sector, or a private company, like a TV station, everything is based on a system that is ultimately imperfect, and in which there's simply no room for people who think. But we all have mortgages to pay off – the people who think for themselves and the single-celled organisms – all of us need to work. The former simply to exist or, at best, to *live*.

I was walking along the street; it had rained a little, and there was that satisfying smell in the air that comes after a rain. It was so pleasant being outside that I felt certain someone I knew was about to show up. And, indeed, someone I knew *did* show up, jumping off the bus in front of me, and I could tell that evening was not likely to pass without drinking.

It was raining, and a bottle of cognac stood on the kitchen table.

'Tbilisi was a relationship,' I laughed, and my friend knew what I meant. We had been drinking and talking for several hours, and I had told him my news. I explained that I thought I'd be able to find some genuine talents, and do some actual good for a change. But now, the way things have turned out, I was willing to do anything for money.

'It's better to do that, than nothing,' my friend said. 'And how long do you want to live off your aunt for? Sooner or later they're going to auction off your aunt's apartment too…' My friend was a geographer, and worked as a tour guide. 'Look at me – look at what I've become… you have no idea the sort of shit I have to deal with.'

'Why? What's happened?' I asked.

'So, the other week, I was taking a group of Jewish people around Mtskheta. I was telling them about one of the frescoes in the Svetitskhoveli Cathedral and was drawing parallels between Judaism and astrology, when one of the women selling candles overheard me, and snitched on me to a priest. This priest then came at me, and started to intimidate me, saying, "How dare you talk about Judaism in an Orthodox temple!" He literally kicked me and my tourists out of the cathedral. The interpreter for the group was going crazy: "What right do you have to kick us out of the temple?" he was shouting. Outside, other people started shouting at us, "You, boy, who brought Jews in here! Here, into this temple! We have no problem with Jews per se – Christ's mother was a Jew – but you, you should be ashamed." They started hurling rocks at all of us, and that's how we were also kicked out of the cathedral grounds.'

I told my friend about the former colleague who was fired for being over-educated; we both smiled bitterly, and poured another drink.

Life is a strange compromise. There are so many issues to address, so many things that need saying, or need writing about, and my job is to find untalented people for a talent show in order to chase the ratings.

We were drinking cognac, and with a gloom hanging over me, it wasn't long before I became completely inebriated.

### 3.

I have no special talent. Since childhood, I've failed to excel in either sports or science. At school, I was neither a leader of the troublemakers, nor a truant, nor did I pick on weaker kids for their pocket money, like some kind of hoodlum. I always spoke my mind. I would criticise the teachers for giving good grades preferentially to those kids that paid for additional private lessons with them, or at least, those who paid for group lessons. I refused to buy the fifth volume of the Georgian teacher's *Collected Poems* because it was expensive and much the same as the previous four. I told the headmaster that he had to fix the crumbling parquet on the third floor for two reasons: (i) so that the children would stop making weapons to fight with out of bits of parquet that dropped into the playground, with nails in, and (ii) so that the biology teacher would desist from gathering up bits of it to feed the stove she'd installed in her office without permission. This was the biology teacher who refused to teach us sex education, saying, 'My husband died twenty years ago!'

Because of my naive passion for 'justice', as I called it, I was forced to change schools several times, and in the end I was only able to graduate with the influence of close friends. At university I studied film-making, but I didn't set eyes on a camera for four long years. There was a rumour that the university owned a camera, but that it was constantly being hired out for weddings. This wouldn't have surprised me. On one occasion, the students started a fight with the professors about the camera, and were promised that a camera would be brought into a lecture in the following few days. A few days later, we did indeed have a lecture about how to use a camera, but what was brought in was just a diagram of one. That was the first day I found myself cursing a man old enough to be my grandfather.

After graduating, I somehow got lucky and participated in a youth project, and produced a short film that did well. Since then I've been working in television. No one has ever said I'm a talented director, or that I had a future ahead of me; no one has even written a single word by way of review of my work. Also, once I taught an art class for my friend, and I was very happy with the talk I gave. But the students told me they were only there to learn about colour schemes and the titles of artistic movements, and, to put it politely, didn't particularly care for my extended monologue on the links between Etruscan frescos and Banksy.

I had no talent for anything, or if I once did, I'd lost it.

Instead, I sit at work all day, browsing the internet, looking for heroes.

But, you know, in Tbilisi, it's really hard. Those who haven't already broken into show business go into politics, leaving nothing for me. And so, I had to go out of town. The best I'd had so far was some Kutaiseli[3] who'd come in to internal casting in the first few weeks. He couldn't retain the lyrics to a single song all the way through, and he couldn't eat glass bottles, either. In short, he was completely without talent. There were three months before the show was supposed to air. My producer and colleagues had pulled down a good number of bonuses for their finds, but at this rate I was barely going to get a salary.

I came across another possibility. He was hitting his abs with a mallet. I brought him to casting, and they actually liked him, but then told him he had no room to develop. They asked him, 'OK, in the first round you hit yourself with a mallet, but what are you going to do in the second one?'

'In the second one, I'm going to hit myself with two mallets. I can even play ping-pong with a mallet.'

'Oh, I can't stand ping-pong,' said my boss's 'friend'. I didn't understand what he didn't like about ping-pong, but that's how he decided everything – whether he liked it, or not. He clearly didn't like me, and had long-since given up on me. 'You,' he said, turning to me, 'have turned out to be quite talentless at finding people without talent.'

I was walking down the street. It was a depressing kind of day, and I was in a frightful mood. Sometimes, Tbilisi can feel difficult and square: a big, built-up mass with no soul, no positive vibrations. Now and then the rain makes it slightly more attractive to look at, but I don't like the place. I was not liking it so much on that particular day, that I could tell someone I knew was about to show up. Sure enough he did, jumping off the bus in front of me, in a sad kind of way, and I knew that the evening would not pass without drinking.

When two men drink cognac together, quietly, understanding each others' problems while barely exchanging a word – this can be a difficult moment. My friend had shared two pieces of news with me: first, he had developed some kind of problem with his spine, from being tired and stressed. 'My whole back is tense,' he explained. 'The doctor prescribed a massage, and I got one from these old dudes, but I didn't like it, and it didn't help much. I asked around, and people suggested yoga or Chinese massage.' There was a pause.

'And the second piece of news?' I asked.

'The second...' He looked thoughtful. 'They fired me. They fired me!' Someone had snitched to my friend's boss that apparently he wasn't acting like a true Orthodox – even though I didn't know anyone who was *more* devout than him! After the incident when he was evicted from the monastery with the Jewish tourists, and had rocks thrown at him, he started to blame himself. 'Maybe I just annoy people,' he muttered to himself. In short, the hypocrites had accused my believing friend of being an unbeliever. His boss told him, 'You told the priests that we have to resemble Christ. How dare you say this? Who do you think you are?' My friend had been startled: 'If a Christian shouldn't resemble Christ, then who should he resemble?'

'You can't reason with these people,' I interrupted. 'Screw them!' He laughed at this, and after that we sat and drank quietly, from time to time looking out the window. There's a city outside this window full of talented people, I thought, and my job is to look for idiots, my friend has no job at all, and while I try to pay off my loans my aunt tortures me: 'I'll make *pkhali* for dinner!'⁴

*Pkhali!*

My friend and I got a little drunk. We ventured out into the city, despite my friend's back pain. He'd found the address of a reputable massage parlour, so we climbed onto a bus heading to the centre. These buses are one of the main problems in this city. For one thing, they're all hideous and falling apart, and for another, there are so many adverts plastered across the windows that you can't see what's going on outside. It just makes you dizzy and gives you a headache. The ticket machines don't work on most of them, even though they were only bought five or six years ago. The mayor of this city is a pillock. If you didn't need a massage before getting on a bus like this, you needed it afterwards.

My friend's hallowed massage parlour turned out to be very close to my house. They'd turned on colourful lights at dusk, and these were a joy to look at. We entered. In the foyer was an Asian woman, and she was very happy to see us. She said something to us in a mix of Georgian and English, 'Massage, massage, 40 *lari*, 40 *lari.*' We gave her the money, and she led us downstairs, into two separate rooms. There was low, soft lighting and a massage table in the room. I took off my clothes, wrapped myself in a towel, and lay down on the table. In a few seconds a gorgeous, thin Asian girl with long black hair came in. I stared at her face. She was my neighbour. She looked at me for a long time, finally recognised me, and smiled. She had the most beautiful smile.

### 4.

It was Saturday, my day off, so I was sitting on the balcony scrolling through websites and video channels looking for talent, in vain, of course. Occasionally I'd get up, take a sip of coffee, gaze into the yard. Nothing was going on. For whatever reason, my neighbours were all settled comfortably in their homes. It was the weekend, so they were getting some rest – from each other, no doubt. Only the Azeri woman was to be seen, hanging laundry out on the line. I like this woman – whenever she makes sweet pilaf she brings me some. I drank real black tea for the first time at her place. She has this colourful rug hanging on her kitchen wall; it's very eye-catching. I've known her ever since I was a child – she used to give me sweets. I loved staring at her rug. If you looked at it closely enough, you could form a thousand different pictures out of its abstract shapes. I would stare and stare. Other neighbours would say she was a witch, and I'd say she was no such thing, but rather the best of them. My aunt was not scared of her. Quite the opposite – they were friends. My aunt told me how, when they were young, this woman told her fortune by looking at the clouds. 'At the clouds?' I asked. 'Yes, you pick a cloud, and liken it to something, and she'll tell your fortune by this.' At that time I really believed that she could, but now I wasn't so sure. These days I believe in collateral mortgages and talentless internet sensations more than in clouds.

Anyway, my Azeri neighbour was hanging her laundry out on the line. There's something magical about the way laundry rustles in a slight breeze. I don't know what exactly, maybe the sound. When the starched laundry suddenly flaps in the wind, it's as if someone's dream has been broken. The laundry lines stretch from one end of the yard to the other, and each one tells the history of a single family. You'll learn more about a person from the clothes hanging on their line than you will from their resume.

Living in a Tbilisi courtyard has convinced me that hanging laundry on a clothesline has its own rules. The order of the laundry is always the same – it's hung by age. You'll never see a woman's underwear on a line. In our yard, this kind of event happened only once. A family was renting on the second floor, and their matriarch would hang up her underwear, which would make my aunt rabid. My aunt told me, as her aunt had told her, that in the villages, in the olden times of the *abrags*,[5] only 'that kind' of women would hang their underwear in the yard. They'd hang red pantaloons on a line, and this is how the *abrags* would figure out that this was a place that could occupy their thoughts and their evenings. My aunt was a walking encyclopedia of folklore.

I'm standing on the balcony, smoking. My pretty Chinese girl is coming out of the opposite apartment. We look at each other, and smile. Since that day, we've seen each other often. Her name is Tsa. I told her that in Georgian, 'Tsa' means sky. I showed her Tbilisi and asked her a million questions. It was very hard for us to communicate. Tsa didn't know English or Georgian well enough. She'd come to Tbilisi with her sister and mother. I didn't know what she did in China, but they came here because their uncle advised it – her uncle has a store here. 'Since we are women, we opened a massage parlour. Our grandmother taught us massage. My grandmother had healing energy, and knew a thousand different ways to heal.' Tsa and her family's massage parlour had a good reputation. 'In this town, most massage parlours are bordellos,' I told her.

She was surprised and upset. 'I don't know many other Chinese people,' she cried.

Tsa has a mole on her cheek, and she's always smiling. Just now she smiled at me, and went outside to hang her laundry. Instead of a rope, she used a thin wire. I'm watching her. I'm curious to see if she's going to hang her underwear. I know it's a strange intention, but I can't avert my eyes. This time, my aunt comes out on the balcony.

'Come in, let's eat some fish,' she says.

'I can't stand fish.'

After supper I called my friend. We went to a relatively fancy place.

I'd forgotten that it was Saturday and the entire city would be out. There was no place to stand, but my friend and I were in a good mood, and we met lots of people we knew. We talked about a million topics, but the most frequent one was unemployment.

'I'm not worried anymore – everyone is unemployed. Where in the hell am I going to find a job?' my friend asked.

'You should start driving a taxi,' I suggested.

'I thought about that, but I don't know the streets that well.'

'You'd learn them little by little.'

'Do you know what I'm interested in? If these people have no jobs, where do they get money for beer?' I laughed.

'They save it,' I said.

'You're laughing, but it's not impossible that these young bulls take money from their families. They save it all week, and on Friday and Saturday they spend it on beer and vodka.'

'I have a neighbour,' I told him. 'I think he's thirty, and supports himself by playing online poker; gambles all week, then blows it all in two days.' There was a free place at the bar, and we sat down. 'Should we have vodka?' I asked. We drank one. Then a second, and a third, and we chased that with beer. Then we ordered a fourth, a fifth. The sixth and seventh one we ordered together. The place was filled with drunk, noisy people, so we went to a place called 'Nowhere Bar'. We were in the mood for talking, and presumed nowhere would be as quiet as that bar.

There we met even more noise. It was an evening of alternative music, or maybe it was just noise that stood in as an alternative to music.

'What's wrong with these musicians?' my friend began. 'There's so much they could be singing about. Social problems, for a start. They could unite and sing their guts out about something real. Even with just two chords, it would be meaningful! What the hell happened to them? All they sing about is their superficial, narcissistic lifestyle?'

'I don't know,' I said. I didn't know what to say. 'Maybe you and I should become rappers, and promote social topics?'

My friend laughed. We got a couple of beers and stood in the corner. Even though the singers that night were guys of our generation, we didn't meet many acquaintances – it was a younger crowd. My generation was out of step with current music. The mood had changed; the majority of punk rockers I grew up with were now working in banks, or even worse capitalist establishments. I know many people who wouldn't even spit on groups today that five or six years ago they were crazy about. I offered some of these thoughts to my friend, but he was a little drunk.

'I want to pee,' he said. I needed to pee too; so we staggered to the toilets.

A woman, a child, and an old man were standing together in the queue. Someone passed me a joint. I took a drag, then passed it to my friend, who took another and passed it on.

It hit me so powerfully I could barely stand up straight. After the first shock, my brain filled with kindness. I looked at my friend, who was smiling at me warmly. Then I asked the person who was standing in front of me what we had smoked. He asked the person standing in front of him, and this is how we got to the origin of the joint. The first person turned out to be a regular junkie – short, skinny, with sunken eyes and oily hair.

'What did you give us to smoke?' I asked.

'Bio weed, and then I added my own ingredients.'

'Which ones?'

'I put tea and cough syrup into the bio-powder to improve the taste.'

# TSA

'This asshole's given me aerosol with dimedrol.'

I looked at my friend – 'Did you hear that?' But he couldn't hear anything. He was too far gone, and chatting with some hipster chick. I looked at him, laughed, and felt my knees buckle.

Later, we ended up in an EDM club with the hipster chick we'd met in the toilet queue, and her equally hipster friend. I was dancing, or really, I was shaking my body meaninglessly. I usually don't like to dance, but the alcohol was helping me overcome this complex. The hipster girl took a pill out of her pocket, smiling at me wickedly. I remember dancing for a while longer, then I don't remember what I was doing, but I remember the toilets again and some guy throwing up. I remember that I had unprotected sex on the banks of the Mtkvari. Then later, after sobering up a bit, I remember panicking that the hipster girl probably had gonorrhea or something, and then I remember being a gentleman enough to put her in taxi home. 'By the way, my name is Alice – Alice Altruist,'[6] she said, closing the taxi door. 'Add me on Facebook.'

I set off towards home. The street was so empty, and it was so close to morning that something amazing had to happen. I looked up at the sky, and there wasn't even a wisp of a cloud. I went into the yard and towards the stairs with my regular, mechanical movement. I looked at the sky, still looking for a cloud, waiting for a miracle. I didn't see a cloud, but what I did see was Tsa against the background of the sky. She was holding a long pole in her hands for balance, and she was crossing the metal laundry wire, from one end of the yard to the other. Then she threw the pole to her mother who was standing downstairs, and she started doing somersaults. My jaw dropped. I was very drunk, and very happy. I was watching this show quietly, and neither Tsa's mother nor her sister could see me. Tsa finished doing her somersaults, and I clapped involuntarily. The clapping was so loud in the silence that Tsa almost fell off the wire.

## 5.

Tsa's grandmother had taught her how to cross the hair-thin bridge. Her grandmother had been taught by her grandmother, and so on… the secret of how to cross the hair-thin bridge and perform the fire tricks had been passed down from generation to generation in Tsa's family.

'We used to perform in a not very popular circus in a Peking suburb,' Tsa told me. 'I remember when I was a child, the big hall would be full of people, but later there were fewer and fewer spectators. In the end, it got so bad they closed the circus. No other circus would take us. My uncle had started a small business in Tbilisi, and he suggested that we come here. When we got here, we found out that a county of this size has no circus at all.'

'Yes, it was shut down several years ago, but it will come back,' I reassured her.

'We couldn't wait for that, it might be years. So we opened a massage centre.'

I begged Tsa for about two days, in Georgian and English, even in some Chinese I'd learned, to come with me to meet the show's producers. Tsa explained that she had left the circus in Peking, and even if she really wanted to, she wouldn't be able to perform well.

'You walk on a wire here,' I said.

'Here I'm just having fun,' she said, 'but in front of so many people it's totally different.'

'You have an amazing gift,' I said.

She laughed. Two days of begging and pleading eventually worked, though, and I took Tsa, her mother and her sister into casting. My boss and her 'friend' went crazy at the sight of three Chinese women running on the wires. My boss gawped, then smacked her silicon lips. Her 'friend' was sitting beside her, thinking.

'Good job,' he told me afterwards. 'You've found something very cool. These people could become real ratings queens.'

They all started fawning over me, promising bonuses. This 'friend' of my boss was unusually interested in the Chinese women's lives, and made me tell him everything I knew of them, to the last detail. As I told him the history of Tsa's family, he listened with an intelligent look on his face, nodding; when appropriate, he would be sad; when it was funny, he would laugh. He was acting so correctly that I should have been suspicious, but I'm telling you, everything happened very fast. After the first casting we started working like horses – decorations, rehearsals, costumes, makeup, coming up with a new biography, to the tune that 'our Chinese had lost their ancestral circus in a Peking suburb and, burned, came here because they had seen our mega-show on the internet.' In short, we were baking a regular lie that regular viewers had to believe in the most naive way. All these chores distracted and deluded me; I honestly believed I was just helping three talented people.

The day to record the show arrived. It was a sham: on the first day of casting, as if by accident, our Chinese friends wandered in; 'found' our show's 'journalists' and recorded a short interview with them. The programme relayed the biography I had written. Their story affected the viewers sitting in front of their TVs, softened their hearts, and even made some of them cry.

The Chinese women were the stars of the first day of auditions. The show's producer and her 'friend' gave me my instructions. After their first performance, Tsa and her family were selected by the jury. We had to do a lot of thinking for the next round. You see, ninety percent of the people on this show weren't even moderately talented, and the rest were stolen from similar shows abroad.

'This year, we don't want anyone to win who isn't deserving. Let's help these Chinese women advance. Or, if not them, then that child-singer we have.'

'Who's going to vote for the Chinese?' I asked.

'Oh, I wanted to talk with you about that,' he said. 'In short, we have to make a super-cool show, and a super-cool show won't happen without sex.' I knew where he was going.

Tsa complained at first, but she'd already signed the contract, and in the end had to cross the tightrope in an almost see-through costume. On top of this, we had special effects, music and lighting, and the show was really impressive. The result of all this was the jury had a hard choice to make: between the Chinese, or a pair of Tbilisi's own acrobats. Of course, it was all staged. Our guys, to tell you the truth, had very little talent, but we still kept up the tension until the end. The people in the hall were yelling and shouting, rooting for the Georgians, but deep in their hearts they couldn't wait to see half-naked Tsa in the next round. Tsa was so graceful and agile on stage that you couldn't take your eyes off her.

We held discussions for three days straight. A lot of money had been spent on the show, but the ratings were still low. Except for Tsa, we had no one with any special talent. They couldn't even find the kind of people who'd make the viewers laugh a lot. Two or three freaks were popular for a couple of weeks, but then they'd disappear. The finalists were clear. The young singer and Tsa would compete in the finals. The owners of the TV channel were unhappy with absolutely everything. With the ratings, with the number of votes, my boss, and especially her 'friend'. They cursed him so much that if he'd had any self-respect, he would have jumped out the window.

For three days, I listened to my bosses being scolded by *their* bosses. For three days, I couldn't leave the station. My bosses, when they weren't being upbraided, spent their time sitting in the office, scratching their heads for ways they could improve ratings the following week. I could take this for three days, but on the fourth I asked for a break to take a shower, and went home.

My aunt wasn't home. My body was such a wreck that even lying on the bed hurt my muscles. I got up and lit a cigarette. Someone knocked on the door. It was Tsa. She had purely neighbourly intentions. She needed sugar, but wasn't expecting to see me, and her robe was slightly open. Involuntarily, I looked at her chest. I suddenly sobered up, and invited her into the apartment. The sugar bowl was empty. My aunt keeps the sugar on the upper shelf, and I had to climb on a chair. I still couldn't reach high enough, and when I stretched my arm to open the cupboard my muscles tensed up badly, and it hurt so much I almost fell off. Tsa was concerned, put me on the couch, and started to massage me. Then I made tea for her, and we sat for a while, talking about the show. Tsa couldn't understand at all why the show was called a talent show, when the people participating in it had no talent. 'I don't know about that, either,' I said. I was lying on the couch and looking at the ceiling. Tsa finished her tea, and got some sugar, but she was putting off leaving.

'How's your shoulder?' she asked.

'Much better, thanks.'

'OK, I'll go then. Get some sleep, it's already late.'

'I'm so exhausted but my brain is so agitated I'm not going to fall asleep very quickly,' I said. 'If you want, stay – you won't be in my way. Quite the opposite.'

She got shy, and said, 'OK.'

'Would you like more tea?' I asked. 'No, no, don't get up. Come here, let me show you something,' I said. I sat her next to me. 'Look up,' I said. She looked up. On the ceiling was something like a rust coloured flying saucer. 'When I was a child, the water leaked from the roof and this image appeared.

We painted the rest of the ceiling white, but left this part,' I said. Tsa smiled, and I kissed her. At first she was surprised. Then she patted my cheek, and kissed me too.

## 6.

I looked at Tsa, who was sleeping peacefully. Before she wakes up, I thought, I'm going to get up and make tea for her, but tea served in bed seemed too banal, and I decided just to stay curled up. If it were sunny, it might be nice to get up, but when it's gloomy it's better to stay in bed. But it would be good to have tea, now. I got up, went to the kitchen and put the tea kettle on the stove. I was getting the cups down when I heard the first shout: '*Shut down this nest of sin! Shut down this nest of sin!*' You could hear a few dozen voices coming in from the courtyard. I went to the window. Frightened, I threw back the curtain and saw a group of what I could only deduce were 'fanatical parents' standing below. They were holding up placards condemning the TV station I worked at and demanding that it be closed: *You Can't Take Away Our Georgianness! Shut Down This Nest of Sin!* I was speechless as I read the placards. I was used to hearing the anger of 'fanatical parents', but why were they making their demands in my courtyard? Tsa woke up with all the noise.

'I thought I was having a bad dream,' she said.

'No, the nightmare starts now,' I said.

'Who are these people, why are they screaming?' she asked.

'They're demanding that we shut down the talent show,' I said.

'Strange. Why are they here?'

'They probably found out you live here,' I said.

'What do I have to do with it?' she asked.

'I don't know, but that's the only reason these people would come here,' I said.

We turned on the TV. There were protests in front of my work too, but with many more people, making different demands. The people outside the station were insisting we 'kick out the Chinese prostitutes'. They were holding up photos of Tsa and her massage parlour. I looked with shock at Tsa, and she looked back, frightened.

'They're complete idiots,' I explained to her. On TV, an interview with the leader of the fanatics started. He was talking about Tsa. 'There's no room for Chinese whores in Georgia. I don't understand how there can be a group of choral church singers on the same show as this whore acrobat. It's a joke, these Europeans want to take away our Georgianness…'

Tsa started to cry; her Georgian wasn't great, but she understood enough. My heart was contracting strangely. Girls shouldn't cry, at least not in front of men. But when Tsa cried, I felt like everything was my fault. If it weren't for me, Tsa would be walking back and forth on her laundry wire, and everything would still be mystical and beautiful. I was the one who'd dragged Tsa into this morass.

I didn't know what to do. The fanatics wouldn't leave for anything. I wanted to curse them for their stupidity and blindness. I was convinced that these were the same people who troll and shame people on the internet, who don't buy bus tickets and destroy bus stops when they're drunk, who urinate in the underpasses and park their cars in the wrong places, who justify the cult of Stalin, and call Russia 'our common faith brother,' who poison themselves and their children with superstition and ignorance.

They called me from work. It was my boss's 'friend'; and when I told him what was happening in my yard, he said: 'Wait there, I'm going to send a recording crew round.'

'Are you crazy – they'll never go then! And how did they find out where we live?'

'It's Tbilisi, it's not hard to find out…'

'What should we do now?'

'Well, we're recording the semi-finals tonight, and we'll need to, somehow, get you to the rehearsal.'

'If we come out now they'll eat us alive' I said.

'Wait there, I'm going to send security, too.'

The security guys came along with the people from the station. Tsa refused to go. She was distraught, and couldn't stop crying. Looking at her, my heart was breaking. Tsa's mother and sister were also crying. Tsa refused to participate in the show, and I was trying to explain that she had signed a contract, and couldn't refuse. If she didn't perform in the semi-finals, she would have to pay a large sum of money.

'Are they really whores?' one of the security guys asked me.

I looked at him with an expression that made him apologise immediately.

'*Down with the Chinese whores!*'

You could hear them from outside. It seemed they had switched banners and slogans, these imbeciles. Fuck them! They really do need an enema!

'You're betraying Georgians for this Chinese whore,' another security guy told me.

Tsa heard this and couldn't hold back. She jumped up and started to pound on the guy. He pushed her against the wall, and then I attacked him before some other security guys separated us. I had to beg Tsa and her family repeatedly. I finally got them to agree with me when I explained that we'd be better protected at the TV station.

We had to shove through the people shouting 'Whores, whores!' A few of them even threw rocks at us. My peaceful life in this neighbourhood was over.

# TSA

We were exhausted by the time we entered the studio. Everyone working on the project surrounded us. Tsa was hysterical, and they were all trying to calm her down. The members of the choir apologised: 'We have nothing in common with those idiots.'

Evening fell, and the fanatical parents dispersed. They probably went home to watch the show. During the day, they had been talking about us on every news program and internet chat room. The show's ratings jumped ten-fold. According to official figures, half an hour before the show started almost a million TVs were tuned in to our channel.

I couldn't look Tsa in the eye. We were in the make-up room, and twenty minutes were left before the beginning of the show.

She turned towards me, and squeezed my hand. She said, 'Don't worry; I'm not angry with you.' Then she kissed me.

Tsa's sister looked away. 'Those were bad people,' she said.

'Terrible,' I replied.

The hall and the area around the TV station were packed. We tripled security in the auditorium. Tsa was supposed to perform after the Georgian acrobats, and we were desperate for everything to run smoothly. Security was checking the spectators carefully, so no fanatics could sneak in with them.

We were on the air. The members of the jury expressed concern about the events of the day. Expressing concern had become fashionable lately, and not being concerned would seem distasteful. The show's hosts announced the first participants. The acrobats came out on stage, struggled to do something complicated with their legs, and were generally mediocre – the jury praised them and let them go backstage. The hosts announced a commercial break, and the workers brought in Tsa's set and started installing her apparatus. I had a bad feeling. Tsa was to perform without any safety gear, and had chosen a very difficult routine.

We got back from the commercial, and were standing backstage. I squeezed Tsa's hand and asked her to be careful.

'Don't worry,' she said.

The judges apologised to Tsa on behalf of the Georgian people. This caused dismay and whistling from the crowd. On stage, the lights were turned off and Tsa started her performance. She had to cross a wire that was strung up at ten metres high, and perform several stunts. She was neither tied on, nor was there a safety net under the wire.

I was standing in the wings, and was horribly nervous. Suddenly my producer came running towards me, with no colour in his face. 'What's happened?' I said.

'Did Tsa go on without any safety gear?'

'Yes,' I said.

'But the wire's going to –'

At just that moment, the wire broke.

I remember the horrifying sound, then shouting, hysterics. I remember that I ran onto the stage, and was cursing. I remember that the doctor put Tsa on a stretcher. I remember that there was a snapped piece of wire, and that I was strangling my boss's 'friend' with this piece of wire. Then from behind, someone hit me, and I don't remember anything else.

Everything was a set-up, from the 'fanatical parents' to the flimsy wire. My boss and her 'friend' staged it all. The only thing they didn't figure into their calculations was that that evening Tsa was going to attempt her most dangerous routine to date.

Tsa will have to use a wheelchair for the rest of her life. My boss and her fuck-buddy went to jail.

The semi-finals of the show were watched live by almost half a million viewers, and a video of Tsa falling had over a million views.

The individuals who made up the 'fanatical parents' were

condemned by the city's intelligentsia for several days, and went quiet for a while. Within days, no doubt, they were back to living their happy lives, pissing in underpasses, getting away without paying for bus tickets, parking illegally on the pavements.

It's difficult to say what happened to me. I hid like an ostrich, buried my head in booze, never thought about the fact that I wasn't thinking anymore, didn't worry about worrying. Occasionally I would remember the most peaceful morning of my last few years, and would cry. I was always crying, drinking, and not thinking...

I couldn't go to see Tsa in the hospital. I was too weak to face her. I couldn't see her mother or her sister, I just couldn't. She was in there, still, confined to a bed. Instead, I drank. Because of me, a girl who once walked on a tightrope would never again be able to walk on the ground.

One night I returned home, drunk again. I had no capacity left to make any kind of judgment. I staggered up the stairs and out of habit stopped next to Tsa's clothesline. I wanted to climb the railing, but I was stopped by the sound of my Azeri neighbour's voice:

'There are no clouds tonight. You shouldn't believe in miracles.'

'That rug you hang on your wall is a flying carpet, isn't it?' I shouted.

'If you believe it is, then yes!' she replied.

'I believe that if I walk on this, Tsa will walk again too,' I said.

'If there were clouds, I could tell you. But it is cloudless, so you shouldn't believe in miracles.'

'I will walk,' I said.

'Try,' she said.

And I did.

## Notes

1. A reference to the alleged plot of Tsotne Dadiani, and fellow Georgian noblemen, to overthrow the Mongol hegemony in Georgia, around 1246. Having escaped capture himself, Dadiani's co-conspirators were rounded up and, on refusing to confess to their conspiracy to the Mongol noyan Chormaqan, were stripped naked, tied at their hands and feet, and left suffering under the scorching sun, their bodies smeared with honey to attract insects (according to one account).

2. From the poem 'Dada manifesto' by Georgian poet Terenri Graneli (1897–1934).

3. Someone from Kutaisi, a city in western Georgia.

4. A thick pesto-like salad made from vegetables (usually beets or spinach), walnuts, garlic, and spices.

5. The term '*abrag*' is used in Georgian for a late nineteenth- and early twentieth-century Robin Hood type outlaw, a truth-seeker admired by the populace and persecuted by the authorities.

6. A popular hipster nickname in Tbilisi. In some groups of friends, all the women will go by the same first name – Alice – but with a defining surname: Alice Altruist, Alice Misanthrope, etc.

# Flood

## Shota Iatashvili

### Translated by George Siharulidze

HE SUDDENLY DECIDED TO destroy the house.

He started with the chairs.

He knocked them over, kicked them, pulled off the backs.

For the more durable chairs, the expensive ones in the dining room, he used a saw.

He broke the legs off with a hammer.

His wife watched him indifferently.

The children were excited. They surrounded him in a circle, asking him questions.

They dragged the pieces of the chairs around the apartment.

When he'd finished with the chairs, he started to dismantle the television. He removed the screws from the back, tore away the wires and stickers, and took out the screen.

The children's curiosity grew.

'So where is Cinderella? And Tom and Jerry?' they asked.

Rezo had explained to them that they crawl through the internal wires and appear on the screen.

'But you took the wires. How will they come?' they exclaimed. Rezo's wife smiled.

'Do you need a hand?' she asked Rezo.

'If you want.'

Nana went into the bedroom and started destroying their youngest daughter's bed.

'Mum, where is Sopo going to sleep?'

'If she gets sleepy, she'll sleep. Kids, stop getting in the way.'

'Nana, leave the bed alone, and start on the dishes. I will take care of that.'

Nana went into the kitchen, and started shattering plates.

'Don't come over here, don't touch the broken pieces.'

'Mum, let me break some too!'

'Me too!'

'Me too!'

'Ok, fine, just be careful... Like this, take this mug by the handle... Now smash it on the ground! Gaga, move over there... good job. Now you come... take this plate...'

'But this is Sopo's plate, Mum.'

'What's the difference now? Go ahead, break it!'

Rezo climbed onto the table and removed the chandelier. It was a six candle, porcelain lamp. There were angels painted on it. He was about to smash it with the hammer when the phone rang.

'Hello? Yeah, it's me. In two hours...? Ok, no rush... Yes, everything is in order.'

Rezo hung up, but instead of destroying the chandelier's angels, took his hammer to the dial of the telephone and started caving that in. Although, shortly after, the angels found no mercy either; they too felt the strength of his arms.

Sopo, watching her father, started crying.

'Don't be scared, don't,' said Rezo. 'Daddy's not doing anything bad,' he said gently to his youngest daughter, but without any result. Sopo started crying louder.

'Nana, come on! I don't have time for this!'

Nana smashed a salad bowl against the wall, kicked Gaga and Nina out of the kitchen, and went to Sopo.

'Sopo, you're a big girl aren't you? Dad and I are having

fun… What is there to cry about?'

They couldn't stop Sopo. Instead, now Gaga joined her.

'Leave them alone, they'll cry and then they'll stop,' called Rezo, who was standing on a stepladder and ripping down the curtain hangers. 'I shouldn't have started with the chairs,' he said, 'I wouldn't have to drag this damn thing everywhere. I can't believe I didn't think of that.'

Nana started tearing down the curtains. Nina got tangled in the shreds. She looked like a little ghost, waving her hands and jumping around. Sopo and Gaga stopped crying to stare at her.

Rezo went over to the bookshelves.

'What am I going to do with so many books?' he thought out loud.

'Do it the Italian way!' said Nana.

'What do you mean?'

Nana ran to the window, opened it and looked down.

'It's already late, there's almost no one walking. Let's throw them out the window, like the Italians!'

'Good idea. Kids, come over here.'

Rezo grabbed a sniffling Sopo and Gaga by the scruff of their necks, and stood them side-by-side.

'Now this will be a good game. I will pass the books to Gaga, then Gaga will pass them to Sopo, then Sopo to Mum, and Mum will throw them out of the window. Understand?'

Gaga and Sopo were crying again.

'Understand!?' yelled Rezo.

Gaga and Sopo, frightened, went silent and stared at their dad. Rezo took Dostoyevsky's first three volumes and passed them to Gaga. Gaga automatically took them from him and froze.

'Give them to Sopo!' yelled Rezo.

He passed them.

Sopo passed them to their mum.

Their mum threw them out the window.

Ninutsa,[1] the little ghost, was fluttering about from room to room.

Volumes IV, V, VI.

Gaga.

Sopo.

Nana.

Window.

Volumes VII, VIII, IX.

Gaga.

Sopo.

Nana.

Window.

Ninutsa was now stomping around.

The Russian literature alone took them twenty minutes.

'We should just burn them,' shrugged Nana.

'You're right, but only at the end then.'

Nana agreed.

Rezo grabbed the half empty bookcase with all his might and pulled it to the ground.

Nana approached their religious icons.

'O holy Angel, attendant of my wretched soul and of mine afflicted life, forsake me not, a sinner, neither depart from me for mine incontinency. Give no place to the evil demon to subdue me with the oppression of this mortal body.'

Rezo snatched at the icons.

'No, not yet!' yelled Nana. And she continued: '... and keep me from every affront of the enemy lest I anger God by any sin; and intercede with the Lord on my behalf, that He might strengthen me in the fear of Him, and make me a worthy servant of His goodness. Amen.'

The little ghost Ninutsa came to stand by her mum's side, and started mumbling and making crosses over her chest, imitating her mother.

# FLOOD

Rezo threw all the food out of the refrigerator. Everyone was hungry by then, so they attacked the food like ravenous animals, sitting on the floor and gorging themselves. Sausages rolled across the kitchen, butter was smeared on the hardwood floor, tomatoes got squished under foot. When they'd finished eating, Gaga realised he could use apples as footballs, and conscripted his sisters into the game.

Rezo and Nana toppled the refrigerator.

Gaga made a goal, kicking a McIntosh through the door in the middle room.

Little ghostly Ninutsa was wandering around, and flapping her blood-tarnished wings. She had cut her fingers on the broken dishes in the kitchen, but hadn't told her mum. She was waving the shredded curtain pieces on her back, and hadn't noticed that the fabric was slowly growing red.

Rezo moved on to the plumbing. He was demolishing the faucets, and sawing the pipes. Water was exploding out, and slowly starting to gather on the floor. As the water level rose, the broken dishes started to float on it. It worked its way between the pages of the books.

The kids waded around with their little feet, laughing, and started splashing each other.

Rezo and Nana knocked over the beds and the tables, and smashed the mirrors.

The water was rising and rising.

Then there was a knock at the door.

'Don't open it yet!' Rezo called to Nana.

'Yeah, obviously, I know.'

The water was already a foot deep.

Rezo picked up a floating book and looked at it.

'What does it say?'

Rezo shrugged his shoulders and threw it.

'The ink has all run. It's illegible.'

The knocking on the door grew louder.

'Mum, someone's here!' Sopo said to her mum. She was playing with her toys in the water.

Nana took a sodden teddy bear from the water and studied it.

'Mum, what's wrong?' asked Sopo.

'Nothing.... O holy Teddy Bear, have mercy on us; Teddy Bear, be gracious unto our sins. Teddy Bear, pardon our impurities. Teddy Bear, visit and heal our infirmities. Teddy bear, forgive us. Teddy Bear, forgive us.'

The bear slipped from Nana's fingers.

Plop.

Ninutsa was kneeling in the water. Her hands were submerged, and she was watching the water around her turn red.

Gaga waded over to the record player, and turned it on. Louis Armstrong's 'What A Wonderful World' started playing.

'Turn it up all the way!' Rezo called to him.

Gaga did as he was told, and Armstrong's magical voice almost drowned out the horrible knocking on the door.

The water was already up to Rezo and Nana's knees.

'We won't drown, will we?' asked Sopo.

The water around Ninutsa was entirely red before Nana grabbed her hand, and pulled her tightly to her chest.

'Ni... what's wrong... Ni, are you ok? Ni, show me your hands... Ni... my Ni. Mummy's miracle,' she murmured.

Rezo put Gaga on his shoulders, and ran around the apartment, splashing.

'Whoooo!' yelled Gaga, excited.

'Are you sure we won't drown?' asked Sopo a second time. The water was already up to her waist.

'We won't drown,' said her father. He put Gaga down, and put Sopo on his shoulders.

'Really?'

'Yeah, really... it's a flood, but we won't drown.'

Nana stopped murmuring, and looked at Rezo.

'It's a flood, but we won't drown.'

Armstrong's song came to an end.

The knocking on the door stopped.

Gaga was wrestling with the leg of an overturned table, and was circling around it, carried by the moving water.

'Dad, go!' Sopo tapped his head like a horse.

Rezo did another lap in the knee high water, and came back to the same spot.

Nana was kissing Ninutsa's hands. Her eyes closed; she was breathing peacefully.

'I think the bleeding stopped,' Nana said.

Gaga was spinning.

'I feel relieved,' Rezo said quietly.

'Me too.'

'Won't we drown?' asked Sopo a third time.

Rezo and Nana smiled. The water was flowing.

## Notes

1. An affectionate, informal elongation of 'Nina'.

# Dad after Mum

## Rusudan Rukhadze

### Translated by Tamar Japaridze

IN THE MORNINGS I was still a daughter - a long hoped-for child born in early autumn. I opened the door to his study cautiously, afraid to wake him up, but he was already sitting in his armchair facing the window. Without greeting him, I went straight to the kitchen, poured some fresh apple juice into a glass, cut some French toast into small cubes, arranged them on his favourite plate, and pushed the trolley to the study. This time I placed my mum's string of pearls, a sort of a 'signpost' to his forgotten past, next to the plate. Yesterday I spread Meda's shawl (his present to her, embroidered with elaborate dahlias) over his headboard, but he didn't even glance at it.

'Good morning, sir! Did you sleep well?'

Every morning I hoped he would kiss me on the forehead with the words: 'Don't be silly, Sallie! How could a father not recognise his daughter?'

'I didn't sleep at all,' he answered avoiding my eyes and pulling one more thread out of his tattered bathrobe.

'Here is your breakfast.'

He looked at the tray, took the string of pearls with two fingers, as if it were an earthworm, and put it on the desk.

'Thanks. Have you already had yours?'

It had become more and more difficult to guess whether

he questioned me because I was special to him, or just out of curiosity.

'Oh yes, I have. I got up early and even did my morning exercise!' I always bragged to him like a little girl trying to impress her daddy.

I left his room and headed back to the kitchen.

After that I was a customer, an irritated client of the health insurance company, phoning to complain rather rudely in a sleepless voice.

'Sorry, Ma'am, but you have to make an appointment with the family doctor in advance,' the stranger's voice explained, then elaborated on the absurd procedure my father had to go through before he could consult his doctor.

'The patient has no family anymore! Can't a single, solitary person consult a doctor?!'

I lit a cigarette and pressed down my eyelids to prevent myself from bursting into tears.

'I'm sorry, Ma'am, but according to the contract –'

The operator's voice wasn't completely devoid of sympathy, but we both knew that contracts were the best means of protecting people from too much compassion. So I brought yet another futile conversation to an abrupt end.

'I understand. Thank you,' I said and hung up not having the slightest understanding of the situation.

Next I was a furious subscriber to cable television, entangled in engaged tones, left on hold, and desperately struggling to get through.

'Please wait... Please wait... Please wait...' Having waited for twenty minutes, my patience was up, and I railed at the operator in a booming voice demanding they restore immediately the channel broadcasting the programme on fishing.

After that I was a diligent tenant who pays her elevator expenses in time.

Then an impatient pedestrian crossing the street before waiting for the green light.

Then a shopper who's always spilling her purchases from her plastic bag as she goes.

And between all these role-playing episodes, which seemed to pass rapidly before me like landscapes through the railway carriage window, I spotted myself standing still on the opposite platform – a real *me* whom I have always been eager to get acquainted with.

My morning chores completed, I went back to my insatiable Dad and set a sports paper on his lap.

'Am I not going to have my breakfast this morning?' he asked, switching the TV to his favourite channel.

I pointed at the crumbs on his bathrobe to assure him that he'd already had it; I even told him to touch his gums with his tongue to feel the sour taste of the apple juice. But he paid no attention to this reply, looking at the screen and scrutinizing a fishing-boat dragging a net deep through the water with great interest, as if he was seeing such things for the first time in his life.

In the mornings, I was still a daughter – an only child, but a perfect stranger to my dad.

\*

On Monday, Rita came early, as usual. Rita's hands were strong, with deep creases at the wrists and swollen, overworked fingers garnished with silver rings. She always took her rings off the moment she arrived, placing them into the crystal ashtray on the dressing-table. I would've preferred to see thinner, paler, blue-veined hands resting on my father's forehead, to see slender fingers gently combing his tousled gray hair. What I'm trying to say is, I wanted Meda, my mum, to be taking care of my poor dad, to be the one brushing crumbs off his bed, talking to him in a soft voice, reminding him of their first date.

One evening, several months after my mum's death, Dad took off his glasses, stared up at me in amazement, and said: 'Sallie, Meda is late today, isn't she?' Two weeks later, Meda – either dead or alive – didn't exist for him at all. Her place in my dad's mind first shrank then vanished altogether, not even leaving the tiniest scar behind. When Dad's grief at her death had become unbearable, I often wished he'd forget everything and live out his last few years in peace. But now, when I see his empty gaze, I wish his Meda died for him daily, leaving him distraught, with high blood pressure, and reeking of the Validol his pillow was laced with to calm him down.

'Listen here, girl. He mentioned Meda the other day,' Rita said, trying to make me feel better.

'Don't talk nonsense.' I had already guessed what her next step would be.

'Sallie, I don't suppose you can give me two months' pay in advance?'

Bingo! 'No, Rita, I can't.' I refused her without embarrassment. 'You know I have loan repayments and beyond those I'm penniless. We're literally starving.'

She busied herself with cleaning her nails, pretending to not care, for her dignity's sake.

'There are some pickles and preserves my aunt made in the cellar,' I said. 'You can take anything you like. She's an excellent cook, you know; they're delicious. Just leave the apple jam and the red plum sauce for me.'

Hardly had I finished my last sentence when Rita rushed to the loggia, moved the carpet aside, opened the trapdoor, and disappeared down into the cellar, panting heavily.

I opened the window, lit a cigarette, and sank back down into my thoughts about Dad: Does he worry about anything? I wondered. Does he dream when he slumbers the day away? Before this happened, he must have tried to share his thoughts and feelings with me sometimes, but I never had any time for him. Now, I treasure each word he utters and thread them together like my mum's string of pearls, forming them into sentences that I recite to Rita, assuring her he has indeed said all this. I had recently been reading a lot about short- and long-term memory, but I was yet to fully understand how people could recall previously forgotten episodes, or order the many threads of memory into a sequential chain - one which stored important dates and events, as well as the faces of those near and dear to them, the smells associated with people – everything that really mattered, be they the actual facts of the past, or invented ones.

I tapped the ash off my cigarette into a flower pot and looked down into the cellar.

'What the hell is this, Salome?! Damn! It's so heavy!' Rita's muffled voice rose up from beneath. When I joined her, she gave the dusty jar she was carrying a quick wipe with the edge of her T-shirt and handed it to me.

'Wow, Rita! These are sea pebbles! Where did you find them? My father must have kept them there. I used to go down to look at them, I remember now. They've been there for thirty years!' I lifted up my childhood, in a glass jar, and held it against the light.

'D'ya want to keep them, Sallie. Or shall I throw them away?'

Such stupid questions drove me mad.

'Don't you dare! These pebbles are sweeter than apple-jam to me now!'

What else could make me feel so happy in the morning?

I unscrewed the plastic cap with some difficulty, and emptied the jar's contents – pebbles kept in water – into a bowl. I remember my mum telling me that the translucent, greenish ones were merely the fragments of the broken bottles that had been buffed smooth by the waves. She said I shouldn't take them for real pebbles, but I collected them all the same. I put the bowl into the sink and turned the tap on. I picked up the pale, dull pebbles one by one and tried in vain to recall why I had collected them, leaving the really beautiful ones on the beach. I remember very well how we spent long, hot days in the Botanical Gardens. Mum always took a basketful of meat pies and a bottle of lemonade with her. She would sit on a rush mat under a Magnolia tree and read a book, while Dad and I strolled through the paradise laid out for us on the small headland till the sunset. Dad was persistently trying to teach me how to identify the *butia capitata* (jelly palm) among other types of palms by the shape of its leaves and its love of sunlight. The sound of the Latin plant names bewitched me, so I worked hard to attach the delicate smell of the *abelia grandiflora* (glossy abelia) with the euphonic quality of its name. 'From the family of multi-stemmed shrubs,' I would say smiling and snatching its white, bell-shaped flower between my thumb and the index finger, shaking it delicately to hear its mysterious sound.

I should remind him of that summer, I thought.

\*

I had been recommended an old photography studio near the Blue Monastery.[1] So, the next day, I searched Mum's drawers for the old slides. Having found them, I wrapped them carefully in a handkerchief, and tucked them into the front pocket of my handbag. I walked slowly along the old street, called at the Tea House, ordered a cup of Casablanca mint tea, looked for the sunniest spot, sat down at the small table in the corner, and took my treasure out of my bag. I held up the old slides against the light, and the world around me seemed to grow dimmer and more sunless, somehow, as I felt an overwhelming craving to return to the past captured on those translucent films – if only for a day or two.

I located the photography workshop easily. It was exactly as I'd imagined it would be: a windowless, sultry room, decorated with fake pearls, hats, and black and white photos.

'A passport photo?' the old photographer asked me without even saying hello.

'No, I need digital images of these old slides,' I answered and began laying out the whole archive on his table.

'I can't do it sweetie, but my son can,' he declared, pointing into the far corner of the room, lit up by a computer screen. 'Sasha!' he hailed, stretching his neck out and looking at a young man behind the room divider.

Sasha, who was talking with a friend on Skype, signalled to me to wait. A minute later he took my slides, wrote down the fee on a scrap of paper, and told me to come back in the evening.

'He can, can't he?' the father inquired smiling proudly at his son.

'Yes, he promised to finish it by this evening,' I answered handing him the paper.

'See young Booba over there?[2] I took that one myself!' The old man pointed to a full length poster of the celebrity.

'Really? It's nice!' I answered giving him the exact amount of money so as to avoid waiting for change.

'You remember his 'Girls, Buy the Pot-Soil for your Flowers', don't you?' the old man smiled, standing up and showing me to the door, humming the melody.

My mobile rang as soon as I entered the office. I couldn't find it in my bag, so I emptied its contents onto the desk. I guessed it was Irakli calling, but I answered it all the same. Each time he called, I could hear my cardiologist's verdict: 'a lateral displacement of the apex beat.'

'What's the news?'

Sometimes when he greeted me like this, I wondered if

my name had slipped his memory, or if he was just afraid to utter my name in his home too often.

'No news,' I said, holding the mobile at arm's length for a moment to spare myself the inevitable, silly comments.

'I'll book a hotel at the seaside,' he concluded, before trying to decide which off-peak period to pick before the summer started.

'Are you kidding?' I said, looking into the mirror and combing my hair.

'I'm booking it. It's decided!' I imagined him loosening his tie.

'I've cut my hair,' I said. I knew he wouldn't like this and hoped his annoyance would derail him.

'Sallie, darling, let's start again from the very beginning,' he said, launching into his third attempt.

'From the very beginning, eh? OK, so let's find a cave: you can hunt mammoths and I'll paint the cave walls! Maybe something will come out of that.'

But Irakli could never listen.

'Done! I've already booked it, so I'll be there the day after tomorrow! What was it you were saying about the caves?'

I didn't tell him that I would actually be at the seaside the very next day, only with another man.

*

After some delay, Rita opened the door. Not waiting for me to enter, she rushed back to the toilet door and leaned against it with her plump shoulder. It needed a special skill to move so swiftly in those huge, ill-fitting slippers.

'You'd better buy dried plums for him tomorrow! I've been standing here for an hour, at least!' she said, nodding behind her with a grimace, while also straining to hear what was going on inside.

'That's over, thank goodness!' she sighed, raising her eyes to the ceiling.

Before I put on my old kimono, so I could feel at home at last, Rita managed to see my dad to his room and help him into his armchair.

'Rezo, will you have some chamomile tea, dear?' Rita shouted. 'Will you? Eh? Rezo, will you?' At times she seemed to think Dad was hard of hearing, and would start shouting to get an answer.

'The cunning old devil can hear perfectly well when he wants to! Watch this: Rezo, shall we have a nice pint of beer?' she asked him, with her hands on her hips, smiling and winking. Dad smiled back and nodded. 'Ah-ha!' Rita looked triumphantly at me, and we all laughed affectionately.

The three of us had formed a strange alliance over those months of co-existence. Rita and I were both strangers to Dad: he could neither remember Rita's name, nor recognise me. Likewise, Dad and I were both strangers to Rita, or were until that spring. As for me, I treasured each day I spent with Dad in that house, and Rita became dear to me as well, in a way.

'Rita, fill up a tub of cool water and bring it to me, would you?' I said straightening Dad's collar.

'Why? I've already washed the floor here,' she protested. Rita always suspected that I thought her negligent.

'Come on, Rita! I need it!' I answered and started combing my dad's hair.

'I washed his feet some time ago, girl! I even added some glycerin to the water,' Rita exclaimed, second-guessing me.

'I just need it. I'll explain later,' I said pleading for no more questions. 'Bring the jar with the sea pebbles too, and then have a break if you want.'

'You're all weirdos in this house!' Rita grumbled, shuffling to the kitchen.

I brought the laptop from my room and began to set up a little cinema in the study. Dad watched me struggling with the cables with perfect indifference. After a while, I managed to link my computer to the TV-set and switched off the chandelier. Meanwhile, Rita had brought the tub and asked me where to put it. I pointed to Dad's feet. Shortly after she brought in the jar of sea pebbles too, then left the room somewhat irritated. I emptied the jar into the tub and distributed the pebbles evenly, pressing them down with my palms. As I rolled up Dad's trouser legs, he couldn't take his eyes off the screen. Looking at his feet with their gnarled toenails, I couldn't help missing the younger and healthier man he once was. His weak legs and thin arms weren't the same ones I used to rely on, as we braved our way into the rough sea. I made him put his feet into the cool water. He didn't like it at first and took them out straightaway.

'Take it easy, you'll soon get used to the cold. You might even enjoy it!' I told him and made him rest his feet on the edge of the tub. I patted his feet with my wet hands for a while, to help him get used to the cold. A few moments later, he lowered his feet into the bowl and breathed a sigh of relief.

I immediately switched off Dad's favourite fishing programme, and instead on the screen appeared the old photos from our family album. The images were accompanied by the sounds of squawking seagulls and crashing waves, as if to herald a lost summer of my childhood into my father's room. I had been editing the showreel together all night, changing the volume of the sounds, the sequence of the images and their duration several times until they seemed perfect.

'*Butia Capitata*,' I whispered when the photo of my dad and I standing under the palm-tree appeared. In the photo I'm wearing a pinafore dress sewn by my mum; reconstructed out of Mum's larger dress, to be precise. Dad has fluffy fair hair and is trying to put on his thick-framed glasses. Neither of us is ready for a photo: we are screwing up our eyes in the hot sun and looking in different directions. I was watching Dad for his reaction, but he looked at the photos without displaying the slightest emotion.

'*Abelia Grandiflora,*' I continued, seeing the photo of my mum posing stylishly beside the shrub with a cigarette in one hand and her straw-hat in the other.

Dad kept silent again, looking at the images with indifferent eyes, but I could see how, on hearing the plant names, he searched his memory, and tried to mouth the words I was saying.

'*Cercis Siliquastrum,*' I said when the photo of me laughing beside a Judas-tree appeared.

'It's going to rain!' Dad said suddenly in a trembling voice. He was at the seaside!

'*Nymphaea Alba,*' I uttered, gazing at Mum squatting beside water-lilies, her elbows popped up on bare knees, her head resting on one of her hands.

'I gathered some shells for you in the morning while you were still asleep,' he said, without looking at me and swallowing loudly.

'*Magnolia Liliiflora, Magnolia Liliiflora,*' I repeated the name of the plant, changing my intonation.

'Will you go fishing with me today?' he asked, placing his weak, heavy hand on my shoulder.

The next picture was taken on the beach. In it, I'm sitting on an inflatable dolphin between my dad and my mum, hugging their necks. I helped Dad to his feet. I wanted him to stand on the pebbles with his coarse soles and feel himself there, at the beach. The sounds of the splashing waves and the squawking seagulls grew. My heart raced. Suddenly Dad's weakened knees began to shake, and he said in a worried, low voice: 'Sallie, Meda is late, isn't she?' Then he nearly fainted.

I put him back into his armchair and started to cry: 'Dad! Dad! Daddy!' My cries were mixing with the squawking of the seagulls.

Frightened, Rita rushed into room and, having spotted my dad's inanimate body, started to weep desperately:

'Oh, what a terrible thing to look upon! How could he pass away so unexpectedly?! Oh, my eyes! My eyes!' She leaned against the wall and buried her face in her hands.

'Enough, Rita! Shut up! You didn't lament so bitterly when he was *really* dead! I have brought him to life at last! Why are you weeping now?'

'Is he alive?!' Rita stopped wailing for a moment. 'Oh, poor me, poor me! I thought he had died! My dear Rezo!' she cried and started to weep even more bitterly, closing her eyes and trembling all over.

We didn't carry Dad to his bed; we simply dried him with a towel, put warm socks on his frozen feet, covered him with a blanket, and left the room. Rita hugged me as soon as we closed the door behind us and began to cry again, this time shedding tears of a different sort and repeating the same sentence: 'I, too, have loan repayments, Sallie! I have no right to stay out of work!' She wiped her tears with her fists like a little kid, stealing a glance at her bag full of jam jars.

I was in some kind of feverish delirium, imagining it was the break of dawn and I had just heard my dad saying, 'Morning, Sallie!'

\*

'Am I not going to have my breakfast this morning?' he asked me, having already had it, and switched the TV to his favourite channel.

He was an old man who fished alone in a skiff in the Gulf stream.

## Notes

1. A 12th-century Georgian Orthodox church built in the name of St. Andrew.
2. Booba: A popular Georgian singer and film actor.

# A Bronx Tale a la Gold Quarter

## Lado Kilasonia

### Translated by Maya Kiasashvili

'DAD, HAVE YOU SEEN this film?' Gio asked me. He rested his head on his hands, as he lay on the carpet in front of TV.

The screen cast a diagonal light onto the floor of the dark room. I couldn't see Gio's face, only his crossed legs, jeans worn at the knees, and a pair of blue Keds with white tips.

'It's a cool one, really cool,' Gio went on in a way that got me interested.

I was lying on the sofa. I turned round to face the TV.

First, 'Studio Canal' appeared on the screen, then 'Focus Features' popped up among blue and yellow bubbles, then 'Savoy Pictures' against the black background and finally the room was filled with a sweet old melody coming from the dark screen. *Uuu-uuu-uuu*, sung softly. The picture showed a dark sky, a burgundy line across the horizon, and a brightly lit city shot from above; a familiar voice started the story:

'This is the Fordham section of the Bronx, my home, a world unto itself. You could get to any borough in fifteen minutes from here, but they might as well be 3,000 miles away... It was 1960 and doo wop was the sound on the streets.'

I smiled. Isn't it funny when your son asks if you have seen *A Bronx Tale*?

'Isn't it the one where De Niro plays a bus driver?' I asked jokingly.

Gio's crossed legs shifted on the carpet.

'Have you seen it?'

'Are you joking?' I asked in reply. I touched a thin scar above my right brow and made myself comfortable on the sofa.

\*

'It's a fucking awesome movie,' Zuriko says, drags at his cigarette, and casts a furtive glance at Mari. She is sitting on the steps, smoking and watching us. Her dyed fiery hair falls down to her shoulders.

Mari is new in our class: she moved here only two weeks ago and immediately made friends with us. She's the only girl who smokes with us, swears and misses class.

Now we're missing geometry. We're in the school's back yard, sitting on the rusty iron staircase that clings to the stone wall like ivy and is only meant to be used in case of fire. The stairs are the best place to hide, primarily because they are attached to the building from the side that cannot be seen from any window. Secondly, because if one of the teachers comes looking for us from the yard, we can see them well in advance, giving us plenty of time to scarper. You can either climb that high back wall that borders with the street or dodge back into the school again. If a teacher comes from the right, you can swing left, walk along a dark corridor leading to the canteen, then take the stone stairs that bring you to the sports hall. If a teacher comes from the left, you only have the right-hand side to escape: across the ground floor foyer with Shota Rustaveli's yellow bust, past the primary classes, and good luck not getting caught by the doorman and the deputy mistress. The doorman is no problem, but the deputy is...

She's a grey-haired plucky woman. The other day she

spotted a group of truant boys and chased them for about two hundred yards, caught two but missed three of them.

No one is going to run away from her today because Mari's here and Zuriko is showing off, as usual.

'I've never seen anything like that movie, man.'

'What's it about?' I ask.

'About Italians, bro, their quarter, brotherhood, the mob.'

'Who's in it?' Mari drags at her fag.

There's no one except us in the back yard – only broken desks and chairs.

'De Niro, Chazz Palminteri, Lillo Brancato, Francis Capra,' Zuriko stretches the words, trying to make them sound Italian, and looks at Mari.

Datuna winks at me and I smile. I'm sure some older guys were talking about the film and Zuriko just overheard them, then watched it, and memorised all the names – to impress us. That's what he usually does.

'Is De Niro a mobster?' I ask him.

'No, bro, he's just a bus driver and a father.' Zuriko rubs his thin chin. 'Sonny is the mobster, and a nasty one at that.'

'I haven't seen that one,' Mari says.

'Wow, it's awesome and you know what the best moment is?' Zuriko looks at us but it's clear he's telling it for Mari. 'Sonny has a bar in the Italian quarter and one day bikers go in. They all have long hair and bushy beards, cool bikes and what not. There are seven or more of them and they get to the counter and ask for a drink. The barman refuses, saying he can't serve them because of their appearance. Sonny appears and asks what the problem is. They say they just want a beer. Sonny orders him to serve the bikers, leaves the bar and talks to Calogero, the main character. The barman serves the beer to the bikers, who all lift up their bottles as their leader makes a toast to the generous bar owner. The bikers cover the ends of the bottles with their thumbs, shake them, and spray the barman with the froth. Sonny returns to the bar, approaches the leader and tells him it wasn't proper behaviour and asks them to leave. The leader is a big, hefty, blond guy, with long hair and a beard; he says he'll decide himself when to go or to stay and tells Sonny to fuck off. When Sonny goes out, the bikers shout at his back to take care of their bikes. But Sonny pauses at the door, takes the key out of his pocket and locks the door from the inside, returns to the counter, faces the leader and says they can't leave now. Then we see the bikers' faces, they look like they've guessed they're in trouble. And then the back door opens, and Sonny's guys appear with clubs and guns, and they beat the shit out of them. Then they drag them by their hair out into the street and smash their bikes, leaving them in the street and walking away as if nothing happened. And as he goes to leave, Sonny grabs the leader by his long hair, lifts his head and tells him: 'Look at me. I'm the one that did this to you. Remember me."

'Wow, that's cool,' I say.

'It is,' Datuna agrees.

'They say Khabuliani did something similar when he was younger,' Zuriko finishes his story. Then we hear the bell and the school is filled with thumping and voices, as the students flood into the corridors for the break.

Datuna, Mari and I rise to go. Russian is our next lesson. The teacher is a young woman, quite likeable; we can sit through her class.

'Aren't you coming?' Mari asks Zuriko.

'No. I've got PE. Need to see someone,' he replies and heads towards the canteen.

We sit on the back row. Datuna scratches something on his desk with a pen. Mari and I talk quietly throughout the lesson.

When it's over, the bell rings, the teacher gives us

homework, and we head out into the corridor. Zuriko is waving to us from the far end, his face ashen, his hands trembling.

'I'll be damned! I'll kill him!' he tells us immediately.

'Who?'

'Kokhreidze.'

'Gela?' Datuna sounds surprised.

Zuriko nods.

'You've got a problem with him?' I ask in disbelief.

Gela Kokheidze is in the same year as us. He's an angular, tall kid, with the heaviest bag in school, shoes as big as submarines, an imbecilic expression, and glasses so thick that if you look at the map through them, you can see people waving back – as the joke goes. He had meningitis as a boy, so he always wears a warm hood, protecting his forehead and the nape of his neck. His mum has talked to every teacher and student, warning them that her son had meningitis and should never be hit in the head.

How can you fall out with a kid who only ever talks about *Star Wars* and actually envies Luke Skywalker for having a dad like Darth Vader, because his own dad is a goddamn paediatrician!?

'He kicked me,' Zuriko tells us.

I can hardly hide a smile. Gela Kokhreidze had kicked Zuriko in front of the whole class!

'How's that?' Datuna asks.

It turned out that Zuriko went to the PE class where the boys were playing basketball, while the girls were sitting on a long bench along the wall. He sat down next to Ninuka, the best looking girl in 8A. Whenever the ball rolled near him, he grabbed it and threw into the basket. It disrupted the game but the boys didn't dare say anything to him. When the lesson was nearly finished, he and Ninuka got to their feet, still talking, and one of the players accidentally ran into Zuriko, hitting him on the shoulder. He immediately recognised Kokhreidze's Darth Vader T-shirt. Without thinking, he kicked him hard, then turned back to Ninuka and carried on talking. Suddenly a painful kick in the buttocks made him jump and gape in anguish.

'And then?' Datuna asks leaning on the window sill.

Then the players stopped and Ninuka stared into his eyes. Zuriko rushed towards Kokhreidze but the PE teacher stepped between them and ordered Zuriko out.

'Fuck him!' Datuna swears.

We wait for Kokhreidze outside, sitting on the steps. The bell sounds. Among the students leaving the building we can see a tall, angular figure with worried black eyes behind the thick lenses that look like a pair of binoculars.

'Hey, you!' Zuriko calls out and beckons him. Kokhreidze turns his head and his deep-set eyes freeze at the bottom of his thick lenses.

'Yeah, you. Come over here,' Datuna rises to his feet.

Kokhreidze stands like a statue on the stairs, then seems to come to his senses and approaches us.

'Don't overdo it,' Mari kisses each of us on the cheek and heads towards the bus stop.

Kokhreidze stands towering over me.

'Follow me,' Zuriko says without as much as looking at him. The four of us turn right, slowly walking down the narrow street.

'This way,' Zuriko pushes a heavy metal gate that has a padlock and a rusty chain dangling from it. A small silver key shines in the middle of the lock.

At the end of a narrow dark passage, we're welcomed into an old fashion courtyard. Old wooden balconies overlook the empty square.

Zuriko lets us go in front of him, then pulls the chain back through the padlock, turns the key and puts it in his pocket, winking at me.

The three of us turn on the frightened and muddled Kokhreidze. With his back to the wall, he stands there unable to say anything. From time to time he attempts to open his mouth but his lips won't obey and his voice seems to be stuck in his throat. His eyes dart around and he's gripping his huge bag so tightly it looks about to burst at any minute.

Zuriko approaches him menacingly.

'Fuck the likes of you! You hear me?'

And so on and so forth.

Gela Kokhreidze stands still, looking utterly miserable.

'Okay, that's enough,' Datuna pulls Zuriko's arm. 'Can't you see he doesn't even get what it's all about?'

Zuriko darts forward and Kokhreidze hides his face behind his bag.

We laugh. Our raucous laughter brings out an elderly woman onto one of the balconies.

'Know your place, you prick!' Zuriko says and hits Kokhreidze in the back of his head with an open palm.

His terrified eyes behind the thick glasses open even wider.

'You can't hit me on the head!' he groans wretchedly. His huge fist comes in contact with Zuriko's nose at an amazing speed, sending him flying to the ground. He falls face down and stays motionless.

'Hey, you dare hit my buddy!' Datuna yells as loud as he can, taking a step towards Kokhreidze.

'No!' I shout but it's already too late. Datuna slaps him across the left ear.

'Not in the head!' Kokhreidze bellows, hitting Datuna's head with his bag with all his might.

Datuna sways as the bag hits him again, this time squarely in the face. Then Kokhreidze grabs him, and throws him onto the ground.

What I see in front of me is his massive back, clad in a grey sweater which shows his bulky muscles that can render one blow after another. I clench my fists and land blow after blow on Kokhreidze's back as hard as I can.

Kokhreidze turns to me. His bag drops with a thud next to Zuriko. I run for my life to the gate, followed by heavy footsteps and equally heavy breathing. I see the gate at the end of the dark passage and I crash into it, painfully, with all my body, and bounce back. The gate is locked. Fuck you, Zuriko! The heavy breathing gets nearer. A massive paw grabs my collar and spins me around. Gela Kokhreidze, the four-eyed Gela, Gela the Imbecile is standing in front of me, but Gela's familiar face has nothing in common with what I see now. His eyes shine menacingly from behind his thick glasses, his lips are drawn in an angry line and his eyebrows have come together in a hostile frown.

'I said not in the head!' he begins and suddenly his teenage voice acquires a cold confidence I haven't heard before. 'He kicked me for the whole class to see,' he says. His shoulders rise as a fist flies noiselessly towards me.

The first blow hits me in the jaw, the second in the belly, the third in the chest and the fourth in the eyebrow. Blood drips on to the stone slabs of the passage and my face is covered with warm, salty liquid. I collapse.

With one eye I can see Datuna still lying on the ground, trying to lift his head and see what's happening to me. The chain clangs above me. Kokhreidze is trying to open the gate.

'Where is it?' he mutters. He remembers and turns to go back to the yard. Between his legs I see that Datuna puts down his head before Gela gets near him, closing his eyes as if he's unconscious.

Gela goes over to Zuriko, searches his pockets, finds the key, opens the gate and steps into the street.

I get to my feet, wipe my face with my sleeve and stagger back into the yard. Datuna is sitting up, dusting his trousers.

'What did he do to you?' he asks looking up at me.

'I think he's broken my brow,' I answer.

His eye is bruised and he's got a large lump on his forehead. I stretch out a hand which he grabs to help him up.

'What do we do now?' I ask and wash my face at the tap in the middle of the yard.

'Now we need to wake up Sonny.' Datuna waves towards Zuriko.

Zuriko is still lying face down, in exactly the same position as when he first hit the ground. His left arm is under his body, while his right is lifelessly resting on the asphalt.

'Hey, Sonny, get up!' Datuna slaps him lightly on the cheek.

Zuriko doesn't respond. I scoop water and pour it on his face.

His body begins to quiver as if it's a fish out of water. Zuriko turns to face us.

'Where is he?' he mumbles and Datuna and I bend in two with laughter.

There we are, in an unfamiliar yard, laughing our heads off. My broken brow is bleeding, Datuna's eye has swollen like a balloon, Sonny with a broken nose is trying to rise, leaning on his hand. The white sun is hanging in the grey sky between the buildings that surround us. And in the narrow street, beyond the gate, Gela Kokhreidze is walking fast, looking at his massive fists in utter disbelief.

# Balba-Tso

## Ina Archuashvili

### Translated by Philip Price

ELENE'S WHITE LADA STRUGGLED up the final incline and stopped at the top of the highest hill in Tbilisi, in front of the ugly building housing the oncology clinic. As I climbed out of the car, I felt in my pocket for the letter that Elene's doctor friends, Lekso and Togo, had given me to hand over to, in their words, 'the most famous surgeon in the department of head and neck tumours'. The letter said *Dear Giorgi, This young journalist has been a good friend of ours for a long time. Please take extra special care of her. Best regards, T. Zhordania and L. Akhvlediani.*

I had already received an initial dose of 'extra special care' back in the laboratories of Hospital No. 9, where the walls were impregnated with the smell of antiseptic and damp, and the huge, reusable needle they used on me made a horrific scraping sound as it plunged into my throat. Just the memory of that hellish place was enough to bring me out in goosebumps.

And now here I was, a week later, about to do it all again. 'I can't go through with it,' I thought to myself despairingly, but once in the doctor's office, I tilted my head back for him obediently. This time, though, it turned out to be the right thing to do: the cytologist working at the clinic used a disposable syringe instead of a reusable one, and the procedure was almost painless, and over before I knew it. The diagnosis, however, remained the same: I was prescribed a three-week course of radiotherapy which would, it was hoped, reduce the size of my rapidly expanding tumour and, in combination with the radiotherapy, I was to be subjected to various further tests. Once that was all over, I would be given a date for an operation.

I must have walked for miles the day I received the diagnosis before I finally found myself back in my own neighbourhood, on the outskirts of the city. I trudged along with my head bowed, following the edges of the kerb, trusting in them like a blind man trusts his stick or his faithful dog. The only thing that penetrated my eyes and my brain, which were as deadened and dull as each other, was the image of the solid, grey asphalt. Out of nowhere it occurred to me that the reason why people were so eager to cover the Earth in this heavy material, which at a crossroads looked like an empty straightjacket, was to keep it imprisoned, forever. Poor Earth. Cruel people.

It came completely out of the blue. We were just chatting away - I think he might even have been smiling – and then, all of a sudden: 'You have a tumour. It's malignant. You need an operation, urgently.' I bet he wouldn't have come out with it so casually if it had been one of his children or grandchildren.

It was already growing dark when I got home. I locked the door behind me, closed the curtains, slumped to the floor beneath the window, and let out a wail. I stayed awake all night thinking, and the thought that troubled me most was that I might soon disappear entirely from the world, without an explanation.

I thought about all the people I loved – my mum, my sister, Guram, a few of my closest friends – and I just couldn't imagine how I was going to tell them about this thing that had taken over me so unexpectedly.

It was when Anna came to visit from our village and I was hugging her tightly (we've never been ones for too much hugging and kissing – I think that was the first time we'd hugged each other since our father died) that I decided I was not going to give in to this disease. I told Anna the same thing that evening as we strolled arm-in-arm beside the Tbilisi Reservoir. She was so happy it was as if I had told her the doctor had made a mistake.

Later, we stood for a long time on top of a sparsely wooded hill at the head of the reservoir, and watched silently as the great, red sun sank gently and unhurriedly into the water below us. That night I slept like a baby, and this is what I wrote in my diary before bed:

*I'm so calm I feel like a child again.*

*Like the summer sun is setting and I'm in the garden, sitting at the foot of the old fig tree, making bracelets from mallow flowers and singing* tso-tso balba-tso.[1]

*Like my dad has come home after one too many drinks, and my mum can finally rest her tired eyes now she no longer has to keep going out onto the empty road to look for him.*

*Like my sister and I are wandering down the garden path without a care in the world, eating bread and cheese, and my grandmother's voice is following us like a guide: 'Bite the bread but nibble the cheese!'*

*I feel as pure and innocent as the ten-year-old in that photo, the one where I'm stretching my arms up towards the blue sky like a little swallow in flight.*

*I'm as content as our dog Batsara, resting his head on his fluffy paws and snoozing by the open gate, which means that everything is in order in his master's house.*

I go to the clinic almost every day. Piece by piece, drop by drop, I leave behind my flesh and blood, entrusting them to men and women in white coats, like sins entrusted to a priest during confession. Then I go back home, torn and perforated. I've already forgotten what it's like to be a woman my age, living a normal life. Sometimes I stand in front of the mirror for hours at a time, staring at myself, aghast. It's like looking at a stranger. I touch all the contours and creases of my face, examining them one by one, as if only now noticing the grey hair that has appeared at my temples and the dark circles under my eyes. Could it be I'm taking my leave of them?

It turns out a terrible ordeal has a great capacity for dredging up long-forgotten episodes. I hadn't dredged them up before, anyway. Now, though, when I'm lying all alone in the radiotherapy room, cut off from time and space, from life itself almost, events from my very earliest days come rushing back to me the moment I close my eyes.

*It's a bright day in spring. I can't be any older than five or six. I am sitting in the apiary in our garden, fenced in by the walnut trees, close to the hives. I sit cross-legged on the grass and watch carefully as the bees, covered in pollen, bustle about by the entrance to the hive. They fly into it, deposit their load, and then fly out again to fetch back more nectar. I can only just make out the voice of my father, calling to me through his veil as he bustles about in front of an open hive: 'Iri! Irinka! The first honey is ready. Want some? Come and get it!'*

*Then I'm holding a chunk of glistening honeycomb in my hands. It's as soft as a ball of cotton, but I don't bite into it. Instead, I suck the intoxicating liquid straight from the open cells and, even though I try to catch it all, it starts dripping onto my chin, running down my naked elbows, and eventually flowing freely over my dress. Before I have time to come to my senses, a whole army of bees are buzzing around my head. Terrified, I run at breakneck speed towards the little burbling stream at the bottom of the apiary to wash my hands and face before they sting me.*

Or this one, from Christmas morning:

*It's dawn. Ana and I are sitting on the bed, still half asleep. We are wrapped up warm in the soft flannel nighties our mum bought for us in the spring, and opening our mouths like chicks towards an extended hand proffering pieces of walnut brittle. From somewhere in the distance, I can hear my mother's voice, still young, and even softer and sweeter than the candy: 'May your lives be just as sweet, girls!'*

Sometimes I have the strange feeling I am a character in a film or a book. The main protagonist in a high-brow film from Iran or India, or someplace. Or a troubled child in a horror movie - thoughtful, obedient, and introspective, with intelligent eyes, black as coal, that light up the dark night like rays. Someone who lives with her ancient, practically mummified, grandmother or grandfather, and feeds her pet snakes milk from earthenware bowls. Or who spends her childhood in hunger and penury, sleeping on a bed of reeds spread out over the cold, hard earth, all the while living in the hope of a new dawn...

I lie down on an unsteady bed on casters with a chart hanging from it saying
*Patient: Irina Kipshidze, born 19...*
*Diagnosis: cancer of the submandibular gland.*
*Hospitalised for the following course of treatment...*
An orderly wheels me into the operating theatre. I am wearing special clothes for the operation: a white shirt with a wide neck, sporty white underwear, and long socks with light blue stripes. Ana and I bought it all a few days ago at the outdoor market on Station Square, together with some purple-checked bedding, pyjamas, and various other small items necessary for a stay in hospital. I am wrapped in a warm blanket, and yet I still feel cold.

I know they got Elene to sign the consent form. I spotted it by chance through the half-open door of the operating theatre. Later, when I was discharged, I found the form in the pocket of my big travel bag. It said:

*In view of the complicated circumstances, we the undersigned take all responsibility for the outcome of the operation to be performed on patient Irina Kipshidze.*

It had been signed by Ana and Elene.

I also know that my circumstances are being complicated by the proximity of my tumour to my carotid artery, and that this is the reason why the doctors have been so reluctant to offer a prognosis. What's more, I have heard a story about a young girl who was given an almost identical diagnosis last year, but did not survive. The tumour had eaten away her carotid artery, but this was only discovered when they tried to operate on her.

The second evening after the operation, they move me from intensive care onto a regular ward. The effect of the drugs has worn off, and my throat is raw and filled with foul mucus. I am in great discomfort at the site of the wound. Black dots dance painfully before my eyes. My ears, neck and throat are so tightly bandaged I can't feel them at all. I raise my hands slowly from the blanket and touch my face. My mouth is so limp it feels as if it is going to slide all the way round to the back of my head.

'You're going to be OK, Iri. The doctors said so. You're going to be fine. It's all over, Iri, don't worry!' says Ana, jumping up from her chair when she sees me move and then sitting down again hesitantly, like a stranger, on the edge of my bed. Her hands are shaking, and to hide her embarrassment or nervousness she starts tucking in my blanket around my feet. I am touched that she has come to see me. It's for the best that we didn't say anything to Mum; if we had, she would be here too, and I would be an emotional wreck. I can feel salty tears rolling down my cheeks and soaking into the bloody bandages.

Although she tries hard not to, Ana can't stop staring at me. She buries her face in the blanket and lets out a muffled wail.

I am already back on my feet. I've even had a look in the mirror. I don't think it's possible for a twenty-five-year-old woman to look any worse. My face is entirely swollen. The nerves near my chin have been damaged, causing one side to droop down – it looks as if they have removed the muscles completely. What if I stay this way forever? I walk back with my head hanging down, tilted to one side like a bird with a broken wing. If I were to walk along the street like this, I expect passing children would probably throw stones at me.

Elene comes to visit almost every day. She sits on the chair next to me for a while, her small, black, leather handbag placed neatly in her lap, and says almost nothing. Just a few words. She brings me fresh juice she has squeezed herself. She gave me some money too. Last time she came I sensed she wanted to say something important. 'Listen, dear…' she started, but then she burst into tears and ran out of the ward. She seems to be taking it all quite hard. My girlfriends – Maia, Irma, Nino, and Shorena – turned up together, pale and scared. Lekso is in Germany, but a few of his friends, whom I got to know when I was still being treated at Hospital No. 9, came to see me on his behalf. They were so kind and warm, almost like family.

Guram, on the other hand, is nowhere to be seen. My heart jumps in a strange way every time the door opens. Part of me is happy he hasn't come, and another part is hurt. More hurt than happy.

On the morning rounds the doctor tells me the recuperation process is going so well I may be discharged at the end of the week. I am so delighted by this unexpected news I instinctively spread my arms out wide and, as a sign of my gratitude, hug Dr. Giorgi like a loving child hugs a relative.

I am spending my last night in the hospital. They have decided I can be discharged tomorrow. Ana is bustling about diligently but silently, packing up my things. As I watch her, I notice with surprise how beautiful she is, how serene, despite all the worry and the sleepless nights.

It's strangely quiet all around. Apart from one or two momentary bursts of animated conversation coming through the open door of the registrar's office, and the occasional jangling of a medical instrument, no sound disturbs the tranquil slumber of Private Ward No. 307.

Twilight from the slopes of Lake Lisi sneaks up slowly and stealthily on the huge windows. Far away, under dull, yellowish streetlights, Tbilisi prepares for sleep. Before long, the faint, lopsided moon will swim out through the clouds and reveal itself timidly to the room. Heat from the electric stove will do battle with the early autumn hoar-frost covering the glass panes, not allowing it to gain a foothold indoors.

Night falls on the oncological clinic – such a fearsome place to those on the outside.

## Notes

1. Balba: Georgian word for Mallow.

# Patagonia

## Bacho Kvirtia

### Translated by Nino Kiguradze

THE FOOT PROTRUDING FROM the blanket hasn't been washed for a very long time. With its scraped heel and overgrown nails, it looks worn out from too much walking. It belongs to Veriko. Vero – that's her nickname – lies sleeping in a filthy bed, the sheets reeking with the same stench of faeces as the rotten mattress. She's sound asleep, and snoring like a man. At times her wound stings her and she makes a face. She reaches for her cheekbones, black and blue from the beating, and lets out a grunt. It hurts.

In this unspeakably filthy bedroom, there is the kind of stench that would make you weak at your knees, then startle you like ammonium chloride, then make you nauseous, and lastly it would make you so dizzy that if you didn't escape, you'd know you would lose consciousness.

It's 6:30 in the morning, still dark outside, but not long before sunrise. It's late autumn. At exactly 7am Vero will wake and leave. She can't sleep a minute longer. Givi is beside her, snoring as well. His underwear is pulled down to his knees and from what's left of his circumcised foreskin, a strand of Vero's black pubic hair can be seen sticking out. Every now and then, he scratches his own tuft of pubic hair, as if he'd been bitten by a snake. This is Givi's apartment; Vero lives with him. Or, to be more precise, she is Givi's slave – in every sense – and in return, Givi lets her have a roof over her head and a bed to sleep in. The very fact that Vero isn't on the streets – that's something.

Givi is a man rotten to the core. He is a regular brute. Correction: he's an *extraordinary* brute: a pimp, a swindler, a drunkard, a former drug user, and a paedophile. He doesn't care who he sleeps with – men or women – and he brags about it.

It's almost 7 o'clock. Vero wakes and stretches, touches her sore cheekbone and groans, slowly opening her eyes. Beyond the dirty curtains, it's dawn. The newly awakened commotion outside reaches through the triangular gap in the glass at the corner of the window. She looks across at the mirror hanging on the far wall, then gets up with a slow, heavy step, and inspects her face in it. For a second her heart sinks – just for a second – then it passes. Givi is sleeping on his stomach, the blanket has slipped off, and his ass, covered in black hair, is exposed to the world. Vero looks between her legs, grabs the toilet paper next to her, folds a piece and wipes. For a little while she stares at the paper. She drops it on the floor and tears another piece, folds it and wipes again. Again she stares at it, drops it, tears some more and wipes. Then she fetches underwear from the bed, and stares at it for a moment, before putting it on and quietly leaving the room. On the way she collects her clothes and shoes. She dresses in the hallway, goes to the bathroom for a pee, washes her hands quickly, then leaves the apartment, descending the stairs slowly. Everything hurts. She takes each step carefully; but her face doesn't give her any rest.

In August, she turned 57. To this day, she doesn't know her husband's whereabouts. He hadn't been seen dead or alive for over 15 years. Their neighbours found their son, Vitali, one day, in the local power plant, burnt to a crisp. It was back in the days when they used to steal copper cables and sell them across the border, in Turkey. Vero's son had snuck in all by himself, broken the lock, and tried to remove the thickest cable he could find. For two weeks there had been no electricity in the neighbourhood, and but as luck would have it, at the very moment he started cutting the cable, the electricity came back on… What can be left of a person when 6000 volts passes through them? Vero's boy, her only son, was 16 years old at the time. He played the guitar, liked Viktor Tsoi, and had grown his fingernails on his right hand. How long had it been since Vero last visited his grave? After Vitali passed away, Vero's husband left for Russia to work in construction, and for a while he sent her what he earned. But then the money stopped, and he completely disappeared. Vero was left to fend for herself.

She is at the railway station now, dragging her aching body down the street. She makes a turn into an alleyway and descends into a half basement. In a room barely 40 square metres in size, they've set up a bakery under a string of exposed light bulbs. There are women making rolls. A big, smutty furnace opens and closes with a creaking sound as the baker slides the dough into the clay oven. Women take strong, salted cheese and wrap it in Khachapuri dough, then ladle it into the brazier. When the brazier is full they carry it to the furnace and after a few minutes of rattling and banging, they remove the hot brazier, now plump with baked Khachapuris. Oil, which has been re-used a thousand times, sizzles in the large pan and makes the basement unbearably smoky. On the stove, potato pies are sizzling. Next to the sacks filled with flour sits an overweight male cat, licking its paws.

'Man, she's here… she's here. Pack up the breads and bring it out to her.'

The short, fat, large-breasted woman calls out to Vero. It's obvious she is the boss round here. 'Why are you late, my dear?'

'It's only 8:05, Nata! How am I late?' Vero counts and then organises the hot breads inside the box. She is no longer even trying to hide her beaten up face. 'Did Givi hit you again?' Stout Nata spits on the side and slaps the salty cheese on the dough. The other women are silent. They only throw the occasional glance at Vero; expressionless glances, with neither empathy nor disgust. 'Five minutes? In five minutes you could have taken these fucking breads to the market and sold them by now! But what should I expect from a fucking whore! What are we going to do?'

'I'm sorry Nata...'

'This is where I hang your sorry!' She points a dough-covered finger between her legs. 'Tomorrow, if you come one minute late, you're fired... Hurry up now! Don't just stand there, staring!' The smutty furnace, black as coal, opens with a creak and looks as if it's sticking out a mustard-coloured tongue. The brazier full of baked cheese-bread comes out, banging and rattling.

'Bread, bread, bread!' Vero is making her way through the busy Tbilisi open market. She is carrying a cardboard box full of hot rolls on her head, holding the edge of the box with one hand, and clearing a path through the crowd with the other. She knows where she should go, where she can sell them fastest. But if someone stops her on the way, she can't let the customer go. She needs to sell them as fast as possible so she can return to the bakery quickly, get another load of cheese-bread and potato pies, then go back again. She has to sell everything, and fast, while it's still hot, fresh and profitable. Otherwise she won't get her own daily ration, and without that she won't be able to return to the apartment... without a share to give Givi, she doesn't know what that depraved man will do...

*'If the world stops spinning, what will happen to us, Miss Veriko?'*
*'Terrible things…'*
*'Will all of us die?'*
*'Almost all.'*
*'And those who survive?'*
*'Whoever survives, survives. But if the earth doesn't start spinning again, they will die too.' The children are quietly laughing. They are scared and at the same time amused. Veriko is standing in front of a world map hanging from the blackboard. She is going over the lesson with a plastic, transparent stick in her hand.*

There was a time when she worked as a secondary school geography teacher, back when she had a husband and Vitali was alive. Then everything changed. Somebody stops her. They want bread. Vero is in a rush, looking for change in her bum-bag; she hands it to the customer, closes her wallet and is quickly on her way. At times, she becomes suddenly aware of her monotonous panting and her heart sinks – only for a moment though, then she forgets about it until it's time to start shouting again. 'Bread, bread!'

*'Children, what is your dream destination? Where would you like to travel for pleasure?'*
*'I would go to Japan'*
*'Why Japan?'*
*'Because over there it's the best. The people are great. They have great record players and VCRs.'*
*'I would like to travel to space'*
*'Space is not on Earth. Okay, children please don't laugh.'*
*'Where would you travel, Veriko?'*
*'Me? I would really like to visit the land of fire in Patagonia, South America. Do you children know where the land of fire is?'*
*'No!'*
*'It is located on the edge of the South American continent. A famous sailor Ferdinand Magellan coined the name. You remember Magellan?'*

*'Yes!'*
'Is your bread warm, woman?'
'Yes, it's hot.'
'Come, come closer.'
*'Why did he name it the land of fire, Miss?'*
*'I will explain it to you...'*
'Do you shrink the bread on a daily basis? How do you do things over there?'
'Shrink what? Why would you say that?'
'What I say and don't say is my business. Tell your bosses to stop being stingy bastards and start baking decent sized bread. Or else no one is going to buy from you. Now, give me two loaves.'
*'When Magellan was travelling around the world, while swimming in the bay between the continent of America and the land of fire, he witnessed one of the indigenous tribe's rituals, and saw they had a fire blazing.'*
'Vero, don't you have any potato pies?'
'Not yet.'
'When will you have them?'
'Give me bread and I'll pay you later.'
'I can't give it you pro bono.'
'Why? Have I ever cheated you?'
'No... but my boss gave me a warning.'
'What warning? What boss? Give it to me. Give me two, and when I pass by later, I'll pay you.'
'No, I can't. I am so sorry.'
*'Then, Miss.... Is the land of fire far away?'*
*'From us, yes children, you have to fly for a very long time. Day and night.'*
'What's wrong with you, woman? I just got started, I haven't sold anything yet and I didn't have time to eat anything at home. Why are you making me waste my words for two pieces of bread?'

'Okay, don't be angry. Take it. I'll pay for it.'
'Vero, what happened to your face?'
'She got into a fight with her sweetheart ...'
*'Teacher, is it faster by plane or by boat?'*
'I've never heard of such a thing – getting into a fight everyday with your sweetheart,' she laughed. 'What a rotten tongue this vile man has!'
'I know who is really vile.'
'Vero, I want some bread too. Give me one piece and put it over there. Here, this is all the money I have.'
'Oh, I'm not sure I have change for that.'
*'Teacher, if you travel to that land, is it okay if we come too?*
*'You can, if your parents give you permission.'*
*'They'll let us! They'll let us!'*
'All right Vero, give me the bread. Girl, what happened to your face? Did you fall or were you kissed too hard by someone? Come visit me some time, have I ever wronged you?'
'Get your hands away from me!'
'Ha! What's wrong, as if you haven't seen a man's hands before?'
'Just hands?'
*'Teacher, is it cold on the land of fire?'*

Vero was made redundant the same year Vitali passed away, as part of the cut-backs. For a while she was able to support herself – with the money her husband sent back. She even worked as a nanny for a family. But when her husband disappeared that's when the struggle really started. She slowly started selling all of her worldly possessions. Eventually she had to sell her apartment. Desperate, she made a deal with some worthless crooks, who only paid her a third of what it should have cost, then registered the apartment in their name, and disappeared. By the time Vero had given up trying to find them, she discovered they had already sold the apartment and had fled the country. Vero was left homeless. At first she stayed with friends and relatives, but they soon got sick of her. At times she stayed at the railway station, underground, or spent the night in abandoned buildings. Then she ran into a former student in the street. The boy was exporting copper and other junk to Turkey and had become a merchant. He pitied his unfortunate, homeless geography teacher and helped her to cross the border illegally into Turkey. There, he fixed her up with a job as a maid, working for a family in some provincial town. At first, Vero was relieved; it was hard work but it came with a room, food and a bed to sleep on. But beyond her board and lodging she wasn't paid any money, and if she had anything to say, her hosts would threaten her with deportation. Her passport had been taken from her and hidden. Then she met Maguli. 'An angel like you is wasting her time serving these kinds of people.' He helped her escape. He took her to Istanbul, and after much fighting, begging, persuading and cursing, he convinced her to spend just one night with an established pimp, Musa. If she didn't like it, he would get her a different job, he promised. For three years Vero slept with Musa, and countless other dogs and vermin. She got used to it, at times she even liked it. Then she met Givi in one of Istanbul's underground brothels. He confessed his love for her and asked her hand in marriage. He promised to return her to Georgia, take her to his apartment, and there she would live like a decent Georgian woman. So she left with Givi.

He beat her on the first night they returned to Tbilisi. 'You were a prostitute for so many years, used by so many Tatars and Christians and now you dare to want to be my wife.' He sent her to work with the rest of his old whores and made her pay a daily wage. Vero's life had been like this since that day. From dawn to dusk she sells bread, and at night she stands by the road to sell herself. Then she drags herself back to Givi's apartment. He takes her money. If he's not drunk he strikes her once or twice. If he wishes, he makes her shower and then uses her body and goes to sleep. Vero tries to sleep too, because at exactly 7am she has to get up and be at the bakery for 8am, so Nata won't fire her.

Carrying the hot bread, the top of her head feels like its burning, and with a broken, strained voice she shouts 'Bread, bread. Hot bread.' At night, as she re-enters the apartment, the stench of a man with an ulcerated stomach, rotten teeth, a drink problem, and a hundred other nausea-inducing habits greets her, rising up her nostrils and suffocating her. Everything hurts; her back, vagina, nipples, thighs and arms. The roots of her hair, her cheeks, throat and heart, her conscience and Vitali's grave unvisited for years…

*'Mum, I miss you so much. But I can't come to you, they won't let me.'*

'Vitali, who won't let you visit?'

*'They operated on my legs and I can't walk.'*

'Now listen to me woman…'

'I'm listening, Nata.'

'Take two boxes of the pastries. First, you'll go to Jumberi's store. Leave 30 pieces there. Then Cilia's. She wants 20 to 25, but she has to give you 15 laris from yesterday first. She knows. Then go to the restaurant. They need to pay what they owe. Next go to Sergei's thrift store. The women are waiting for you. After that go to the open market. Do you understand?'

'Yes, I understand'

*'Mum, don't be afraid. They glued legs from the chair to my stumps but I can't walk yet. It still hurts.'*

'Oh my! What's this Vitali?'

*'Don't cry…'*

'Oh god, what's this!'

'Are you going to remember everything? Hey, look here!'

'Yes, yes Nata. Don't worry.'

*'At first it would hurt, they said. Then you'll get used to it. So I am enduring the pain.'*

'Why should I be worried? You bitch! You should be the one worried.'

*'Vitali, what's wrong with your hands?'*

*'Mum, why aren't you coming to visit me anymore? What happened?'*

*'What's wrong with your hands, Vitali… are they dirty… what's on your hands?'*

*'Don't cry.'*

'Fine. I won't. What's wrong with your hands!'

'Will you feed me Khachapuri?'

'I will give anything. Eat son.'

'No, I don't really want it. Come visit me. I have chair legs and soon I'll start walking. First the pain has to stop.'

'What are the stains on your hands, Vitali?'

'Some guts and some blood, Mum…'

'Is the Khachapuri hot ma'am?'

'Yes, yes. How many would you like?'

'How much are they?'

*'Vitali, whose guts and blood?'*

'I don't know Mum, it's always like this. I can't get rid of it.'

'One and a half *laris*.'

'Give me two.'

*'Mum, I miss you.'*

'Here you go. I'll just get you your change.'

*'I miss you too.'*

'Did you say something to me?'

*'I love you Mum.'*

*'I love you too.'*

'What is this woman saying? Give me my change.'

'Just a minute. Sorry.'

*'Don't forget chair legs, Mum…and don't cry.'*

*'I won't cry.'*
'Don't cry.'

Vero's whole body crashes into the table, which is laden with gnawed chicken bones, dirty dishes, empty food cans, vodka bottles, ashtrays full of burned cigarette butts and other filthy residue. The table breaks in half and Vero plunges to the kitchen floor. Her bloody face is covered with ash. She is coughing and trying to stand up but Givi won't let her. He grabs the back of a wooden chair and with all his strength smashes it on her body. Vero is screaming from the pain, feebly pulling at his trousers trying to stop him but she doesn't have the strength. Givi is shouting, kicking her between the legs. Vero spits the blood from her mouth, keeping hold of his trousers with one hand, while trying to remove a splintered piece of chair from her hip with the other.

'Vero, give me my money, or I won't let you out from under this table. I swear!'

'I don't have any money left, Givi…'

'Where is the money, bitch?'

Givi wipes the drool off his chin with his sleeve and feels for the gun in the back of his belt.

'Grave…'

'What grave, you bitch?! I'll be damned if I don't make you cradle your own brain in your arms!'

Givi grabs the gun from his belt and strikes Vero over the head with the barrel a couple of times.

'What did you do with the money? You beggar!'

Vero lets go of Givi's trousers and with both hands removes the piece of wood from her side, wiping the blood from her eyes as she does so. She looks at the exposed light bulb, smiling.

'For Vitali's grave…'

Givi backs up, loads his gun and steps forward ready to

unload. Suddenly he slips on Vero's blood and falls neck-first onto the broken chair leg. Vero is lying on the floor, still looking at the light bulb; she feels Givi's warm blood on her arm and for a second she hears his rattling. The light bulb on the ceiling starts flickering. The lights turn on and off, on and off, on and off. Eventually it switches off, and doesn't come back on again.

The ocean is steaming. Everything around is still from the freezing cold. Above one of the icebergs, albatrosses circle the air before landing. Far away, across the bay, sharp, sheer glaciers are showing their tops covered with snow, like shark's teeth. On the ocean coast, penguins have gathered. The birds are shaking their heads and flapping their short wings. All around there is not a sound to be heard from anyone; only penguins, albatrosses, the ocean's steam and the quiet, frozen iceberg. In Patagonia, winter is about to arrive.

In Tbilisi, winter is about to arrive too. On the streets, by the railway station, people are walking up and down. Woman, child, student, merchant, homeless, vagabond, prostitute, drunkard, stray dog, police man, soldier… some are leaving, others are returning. Some don't want to go anywhere in particular… others are sick of everything. Some are hungry. It's life. From the half basement a fat woman with a white apron lazily makes her way out. She is holding a ripped cardboard box. She goes to the uncovered container, already full of rubbish, and drops the box inside. She lazily returns to the bakery. From the bakery, the furnace's crackling and banging can be heard. The box that has been thrown in the garbage bears a dark mark from having been carried on a head.

# About the Authors

**Ina Archuashvili** was born in 1969. In 1995 she graduated from the Georgian Philology Department of Ivane Javakhishvili, Tbilisi State University. From 1995 she worked for newspapers and magazines *Kavkasioni, HOT Chocolate* and *Arili*. From 1999-2002 she taught Georgian language and literature at School no. 6. Her stories have been published in various periodicals, including *Literaturuli Palitra, Literatura* (*Hot Chocolate* literary supplement), *Kartuli Mtserloba, Chveni Mtserloba* and *Literaturuli Gazeti*. Her first collection of short stories was published in 2010 by Saari Publishers. She received 3rd prize in the 2010 Pen Marathon (the special prize of Rezo Inanishvili) and was also nominated for the 2011 SABA Prize. In 2013 she participated in the Literary Seminar for writers and translators in Lithuania. Her collection of novellas *He Was Called Watanabe* was shortlisted for the SABA Prize in The Years Best Prosaic Collection category.

**Gela Chkvanava** was born in 1967, in Sukhumi. After finishing school, he was recruited into the army and assigned to an anti-missile unit in Leningrad (now St. Petersburg). After military service Chkvanava returned to Sukhumi and studied philology at Sukhumi University. The armed conflict broke out in Abkhazia when he was still a student. Everything he wrote before the war was abandoned in Sukhumi and destroyed when his house was burnt down. To distract himself from the war, and to gain experience in creative writing, he began work on several stories set in peacetime. His first success was in 2002, in the Pen Marathon literary contest organised by Diogene Publishers. Since then, Gela's works have been published in Georgia regularly. Russian translations of Chkvanava's short stories have appeared in St. Petersburg literary magazines, such as *Neva* and *Kreshchatiki*. His debut book titled *Local Colours* won him a SABA Prize in 2005. Gela Chkvanava has won several literary awards and is regarded as one of the best modern Georgian writers.

**Erekle Deisadze** was born in Kutaisi in 1990. In 2008 he entered the Shota Rustaveli Theatre and Cinema University, studying documentary and film direction. In 2010 his debut collection *Secret Fuck-Up* was published, and aroused much controversy. There were motions demanding that the book be banned, and, because of the aggression in certain social circles, for a considerable period Deisadze had to go into hiding. In 2013 he published his novel *The Cleaner*, which was nominated for a SABA literary prize award for the Best Novel of the Year. In 2015 his novel *Russian School Holidays*, about the Russian-Georgian war, was released. Deisadze writes both poetry and music. In 2015 his first musical album *Walk* was released. He has recorded some ten music videos, one of which, 'What Daddy Wants', was named by an international jury of Electronauts 2014 as the year's best video.

Born in 1966, **Shota Iatashvili** is a famous poet, fiction writer, translator and art critic. He made his debut as a poet in 1993 with *The Wings of Death*, and since then has published a significant number of poetry collections, four works of prose and a book of literary criticism, which won a SABA literary prize for Best Criticism of the Year. Iatashvili has also translated and introduced to Georgian readers *Styles of Radical Will* by Susan Sontag and an anthology of American poets. From 1993-97, he worked as an editor at the Republic Centre of Literary Critics (on the literary newspapers *Rubikoni* and *Mesame Gza*). He was an editor-in-chief of the newspaper *Alternative* issued by the Center for Cultural Relations –

Caucasian House and later became the editor of the publishing house Caucasian House. Currently, he is an editor-in-chief of the journal *Akhali Saunje* and leads the rubric 'Library' at Radio Liberty. Iatashvili has won several poetry awards and is the participant of numerous international literary festivals. His poems have been published in several countries, among them the UK, Ukraine, Germany, Russia, Azerbaijan and the Netherlands.

**Dato Kardava** (the pseudonym of Jimsher Rekhviashvili) was born in 1968. He graduated in 1992 from Tbilisi State University's physics faculty. For over twenty years he has been a working journalist and at the same time writing prose works. His first stories were published in the magazine *Arili* in the 1990s. Since 2002 he has been a reporter and blogger at the Tbilisi office of Radio Liberty. His first prose collection *Noah's Doves* was published in 2005, and in 2011, his extended essay *A Toilet Reader*. Both books were nominated for the SABA literary prize. He has won several other prizes for journalism and literature. In 2011 a story of his was included in the anthology *21st Century Georgian Short Stories*. In 2013 he published a collection of essays about the River Mtkvari, *The Mtkvari and its Two Banks*.

**Lado Kilasonia** was born in 1985. He studied rugby in Durban, South Africa, at the Sharks Rugby Club academy, and graduated from Tbilisi State University in 2007. At the same time he was a trainer for Georgia's 19- to 20-year-old rugby players' team, and a member of Georgia's rugby development group and national academy. He was four times European champion: in 2005, as a player; in 2011, 2013 and 2014 as a trainer. At the same time, he wrote articles on rugby for various sports and general newspapers and magazines. He has written seven books. His works have been published in Georgian literary journals and newspapers Kilasonia's short stories have been translated into Russian, Polish and Lithuanian and shortlisted for the SABA literary prize 2008-2014.

**Zviad Kvaratskhelia** was born in 1986. He graduated from the Faculty of Jurisprudence at Shota Meskhia Zugdidi State Institute. In 2008 Zviad Kvaratskhelia started to work as an art editor of the magazine *Premieri* and later, through 2010-2011, he was a deputy editor of the magazine *Kartuli Mtserloba* (Georgian Writing). At present the author works at the publishing houses Intelekti and Artanuji as coordinator of publication projects and as an editor. He is the author and editor in-chief for several publication projects, and has blogged for *Mastsavlebeli.ge* since 2013. Kvaratskhelia has also published short stories, miniatures and literary-documentary essays in Georgian periodicals, as well as story collections. In 2016 his first novel *Form No. 100* won a SABA literary prize for Best Novel of the Year.

**Bacho Kvirtia** (b. 1974) is a writer, playwright and screenwriter, who graduated from Tamaz Chiladze's Studio at the Rustaveli Film and Theatre University in 1996. His prose has been published in various Georgian periodicals. In 2011-2012 he participated in the Royal Court Theatre two-year project New Writing, organised by the British Council Tbilisi and the Tumanishvili Foundation. His prose collections include: *Before the Train Comes In* (2007), *The Call of the Sleeping Cyclops* (2011) and *The Tasmanian Tiger* (2013). Kvirtia is the recipient of many literary awards, including the Pen Marathon award; the Tsero (Heron) award (2007); the SABA prize for the Best Prose Debut (for the collection *Before the Train Comes In*, 2008); Guram Rcheulishvili Prize Alaverdi for the Best Short Story (2011). In 2011, he became

## ABOUT THE AUTHORS

a member of the Georgian PEN-Club. His debut novel *Inga's Corduroy Jacket* (Intelekti Publishing) was published in 2017.

**Iva Pezuashvili** was born in 1990. He is a contemporary Georgian writer and screenwriter, and in 2011 graduated from the Feature Film Department of Shota Rustaveli Cinema and Theatre University. In the same year, he won the Autumn Legend, a student literature competition, with his story 'Alchu' (Lucky Toss). In 2012 he made a film, *Babazi*, based on the story. He is the author of several TV documentary films. He has been publishing his stories in periodicals since 2012. Since 2014 he has been a scriptwriter for the film series *Tiflis*. Intelekti published his debut book *I Tried* in 2014.

**Rusudan Rukhadze** (born 1974) graduated from the History Department of Ivane Javakhishvili, Tbilisi University, and completed her MA in Media Management and Journalism at GIPA in 2008. She has worked for numerous periodicals since 1996, and her first story *The Morning Before Christmas* was published in *Literaturuli Gazeti* in 2013. In 2014, Intelekti released a collection of her published stories called *Tea-Time Stories*. The book includes *Ada and Eve*, which won third prize in the Tsero literary competition. It was also included in the annual selection of The Best 15 Stories published by Bakur Sulakauri, and nominated for the 2014 SABA prize for the Best Debut. Rukhadze won the literary SABA prize for her second book *One of You Betrays Me* in the Best Prose Collection category in 2017.

# About the Translators

**Mary Childs** is a lecturer at the University of Washington, in Seattle, Washington, in the Comparative History of Ideas program, where she teaches courses on the Black Sea Region, Georgian literature and culture, and Environmental Humanism. She has travelled throughout many, though not all, regions of Georgia over the past decade. She has been writing about and translating Georgian literature for several years, and is honoured to have some of her translations published in the current volume.

Dr. **Tamar Japaridze** was born May 1, 1955 in Tbilisi, Georgia. She is the Founder of St. George's British-Georgian International School in Tbilisi and former Professor of the Tbilisi State University (Department of the English Language and Literature). Tamuna is also presenter and author of two educational TV programs: *TV English* and Home School, author of 4 books and 17 publications on English Philology, and 16 school text-books of English. She is also the translator of 26 literary works from English into Georgian, and 22 from Georgian into English and was awarded the SABA prize for the Best Translation of the Year in 2016.

**Maya Kiasashvili** (born 1954) is a graduate of Tbilisi State University with a Ph. D. in linguistics, where she has been teaching English for most of the time. More than teaching, teacher training and being a team leader for Speaking Examiners of Cambridge Exams in three centres in Georgia, she enjoys translating novels, plays, short stories and screenplays from Georgian to English. One of her translations – Lasha Budghadze's *The Navigator* was the winner of the BBC

## ABOUT THE TRANSLATORS

Playwriting 2011 Competition in English as a First Language category. Her translations of the novels by two modern Georgian writers – Lasha Bughadze's *The Literature Express* and Tamaz Chiladze's *The Brueghel Moon* – were published by Dalkey Archive Press in 2013 and 2014. She also completed her late father's, Nico Kiasashvili's translation of James Joyce's *Ulysses*, preparing it for publication in 2012.

**Nino Kiguradze** received a BA in English from Oklahoma State University and is currently finishing an MA in English at the City College of New York. She worked as an interpreter in summer of 2008 at the Vaziani army base and took a translation workshop in 2016 at CCNY. This is her first published translation.

**Philip Price** studied German and Russian at Glasgow University, then moved to Tokyo, where he currently works as a full time Japanese-English translator. He started studying Georgian several years ago as a hobby, and quickly grew to love the language, literature, and culture of Georgia. These are his first Georgian translations to be published.

**George Siharulidze** was born in Tbilisi, Georgia in 1990, and moved to the United States when he was just three years old. He earned his Bachelor's Degree in Psychology from Boston University, and studied screenwriting at the New York Film Academy. Today, when George isn't developing his own screenplays or short stories, he translates Georgian literature, working to bridge the two halves of his identity.